I turned my head and peeked into the guest room, not wanting to go inside again.

My heart stopped.

A glossy black bat flew in through the open window and balanced on the sill. The bat's eyes were trained on the other bats in their cages. Like clockwork, all the bats in the room began unfolding their wings and opening their eyes, waking up. They even yawned, revealing pointy fangs.

And then —

The bat on the windowsill began to transform. The wings disappeared and were replaced by long, graceful arms. The squat, furry body lengthened out and began to take on a human form. As I stared, my eyes growing wider, my pulse pounding at my throat, the tiny bat head began to morph into a human face. A *familiar* human face.

POISON APPLE BOOKS

This Totally Bites!

by Ruth Ames

SCHOLASTIC INC.

New York   Toronto   London   Auckland
Sydney   Mexico City   New Delhi   Hong Kong

Thanks to: AnnMarie Anderson, Becky Shapiro, Abigail McAden, Yaffa Jaskoll, and everyone at Scholastic for ensuring that this book didn't bite; my dear friends, for putting up with my wild imagination; and my amazing family, for telling me stories about the Carpathian Mountains.

ISBN 978-0-545-25840-1

12 11 10 9 8 7 6 5 4 3 2   10 11 12 13 14 15/0

Printed in the U.S.A.   40
First Scholastic Book Clubs printing, March 2010

For my grandmother, Margaret

Love always

Chapter One

The room was ice-cold and pitch-black.

I tiptoed inside, my heart thudding. The silence seemed to swallow me. I glanced over my shoulder, hoping no one had followed me. It looked like I was alone. I wiped my clammy palms against my satin skirt and took a deep breath.

Then I saw them.

Glowing from every corner, like tiny points of light, were pairs of small red eyes. Evil eyes. And they were staring right at me.

Fear snaked down my spine, but I told myself not to run away. I had to go ahead with this. There was no turning back now.

Suddenly, an eerily familiar voice called out in the darkness.

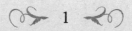

"Emma-Rose!"

I froze. They knew my *name*?

The familiar voice called again, more urgently this time.

"Emma-Rose! Up and at 'em, young lady!"

Wait, what?

I blinked, and another room materialized before me. Purple curtains. Black wallpaper dotted with hot-pink skulls. A picture I'd drawn of my best friend, Gabby, tacked up over a wooden desk . . .

Oh.

I was in my bedroom. And my mother was hovering over me, frowning. My heartbeat slowed down as reality sank in.

It was Mom who'd been calling my name. I'd been *dreaming*.

Having that same creepy nightmare. Again.

"It's after seven, honey," Mom said, glancing at my bedside alarm clock. I must have slapped the OFF button in my sleep. "You can't keep being late for school."

"I know," I groaned, sitting up and brushing my dark hair out of my eyes.

Ever since I turned twelve in August, I've had serious trouble falling asleep. I'll toss and turn, my

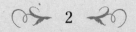

thoughts tumbling, and I won't drift off until dawn. And lately, my dreams had been haunted by those glowing red eyes.

Yawning, I watched as Mom walked over to my window and yanked up the shade. I cringed — but then felt a swell of relief. It was a beautiful day. The sky over Central Park was a stormy gray, the autumn wind howled, and thunder rumbled. I smiled, suddenly feeling awake and alert.

Okay. I realize that most people — say, my parents, and Gabby, and pretty much anyone normal — prefer warmth and sunshine. But gloomy weather suits me best. I guess I've always felt a little bit different from other people, period.

Her mission accomplished, Mom headed for the door. "Sausages and eggs for breakfast!" she sang over her shoulder as she left.

My stomach growled. The promise of sausages (and rain) made it easier than usual to get out of bed. I padded across my room, my black shag rug tickling my bare feet. Mom and I had fought long and hard over that rug; she hadn't understood why I didn't want a cheerful yellow one instead. Thankfully, Dad had said it was important for me to express myself creatively, and I'd agreed. I want to be a designer when I grow up — maybe fashion, or interiors, or both.

After showering, I put on one of my favorite outfits: a black sweater dress, dark purple tights, and knee-high black boots. Then I joined my parents in our too-bright kitchen. Mom was brewing coffee, and Dad was eating cereal while he watched New York 1, the local news channel. Outside, eight stories down, Manhattan bustled to life with the blare of taxicab and bus horns.

"Oh, honey," Mom sighed, eyeing my dress as she handed me a plate of sausages, scrambled eggs, and toast. "Won't you at least *try* wearing pastels one day?"

My parents love pastels. That morning, Mom had on a light blue pantsuit, and Dad wore a white T-shirt and khakis. But the differences between me and my parents go beyond our taste in clothes. I don't resemble either of them — at all. Mom is blond with gray eyes, Dad has auburn hair and brown eyes, and they both tan easily. I have long, straight jet-black hair, navy blue eyes, and milk-pale skin that turns a lovely shade of flaming lobster after two minutes in the sun. Gabby likes to joke that I was adopted, and I've wondered about that myself.

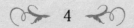

"Hmm," I replied, plopping down next to Dad at the small table. "Pastels. Let me see. Maybe . . . when pigs fly?"

"Good morning to you, too, Ms. Snarky." Dad flicked off the news and smiled at me, wiggling his reddish eyebrows. "Don't give your mother a hard time," he chided me gently. "She's got a busy Monday ahead of her." Dad is a cartoonist, and he works from home, so he's usually the more laid-back parent.

Mom nodded, pouring coffee into her silver thermos. "We're putting the final touches on the Creatures of the Night exhibit. The opening's only two weeks away."

I felt a beat of excitement as I dug into my breakfast. Mom works at the American Museum of Natural History, which is a few blocks from our apartment building. The museum is most famous for its dinosaur bones, but it also hosts cool exhibits on things like butterflies and sea monsters. Mom is in charge of these exhibits, and every time one opens, she and Dad go to a big party at the museum. This year, for the first time, Mom was allowing me to attend the opening gala, too. I couldn't wait.

"And, of course, our special guest is arriving this

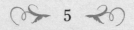

afternoon," Dad said, standing up and putting his bowl in the sink.

"Guest?" I repeated, glancing from Dad to Mom in confusion. Just then, our shaggy sheepdog, Bram, came bounding into the kitchen with a series of barks. When I reached down to pet him, he veered away from me. Sigh.

"You don't remember?" Mom asked, stepping around Bram and checking the screen of her iPhone. "Your great-aunt Margo is coming to stay with us, all the way from Romania. She's been a long-distance consultant on the exhibit, and now she's going to help out with the opening."

Right. I did recall hearing about Great-aunt Margo, my mom's aunt, who still lived in the small European town that Mom is originally from. My dad was born in New York City, like me, but Mom came over to America with her parents when she was a baby. I was really little when my grandparents died, so I knew basically nothing about my European heritage.

I was about to ask how, exactly, Great-aunt Margo would be helping, when the doorbell rang. Bram starting barking like crazy, and my parents and I looked at one another. "Gabby," we said at the same time.

Every morning, Gabby comes to pick me up so we can walk to school together. Unfortunately, she often ends up going ahead without me because I can't wake up on time. Gabby is extremely punctual.

"I'll let her in on my way out," Mom said. "See you later, guys!" She kissed Dad, hugged me, and whooshed out of the kitchen.

A second later, Gabby appeared, her honey-colored curls spilling over the front of her green cardigan. Bram jumped on her, his tiny claws digging into her jeans as his tail wagged frantically. It's sad but true: My dog hates me and loves my best friend.

"Hey, cutie," Gabby said to Bram, rubbing behind his ears. "Morning, Mr. Paley!" she greeted Dad, who waved to her from where he stood at the sink. Then Gabby turned to me, her dark eyes dancing. "I *knew* you'd be ready this morning, Em," she said. "It's your kind of weather."

Gabby gets me. She's gotten me ever since the first grade, when I was the only kid who wanted to

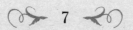

stay inside and draw during recess. One day, without any fuss, Gabby walked away from the monkey bars and the dodgeball games, sat down next to me, and started to draw, too. And the thing is, Gabby *likes* sports and running around outside. But she'd simply decided that I needed someone to keep me company. So we drew and drew, and by the end of recess, we were inseparable.

We still are. Gabby lives about five minutes away, and if I'm not at her place, she's at mine. We'll spend hours painting each other's nails (mine black, Gabby's purple), downloading music, swapping cuff bracelets, and talking, talking, talking. We have other good friends — like Padma Lahiri and Caitlin Egan, with whom we eat lunch every day — but I don't feel as bonded to them. I'm an only child, and Gabby is totally my stand-in sister.

"Hang on. I'm almost done," I said, my mouth half-full as I wolfed down the remains of my sausage.

"Pace yourself, Emma-Rose!" Dad called as he scrubbed the breakfast pans.

Gabby shook her head at me. "I don't know *how* you can eat that stuff."

Gabby is a vegetarian, and usually she puts up

with my burger cravings just like I put up with her salads. But my BFF *can* be a bit annoying when she starts gushing about the wonders of bean sprouts.

"It's easy," I replied, reaching for my glass of cranberry juice. "You know, open mouth, insert food, chew. I can get you some tofu to practice on."

Gabby stuck out her tongue at me, and then we both burst out laughing. Dad looked at us like we were insane, which only made us laugh harder. When we finally calmed down, I put my plate in the sink and slung my backpack over my shoulder. Then Gabby and I said good-bye to Dad and to Bram (who flat-out ignored me), and took off.

As we rode down in the creaky old elevator, Gabby faced me, her eyes wide.

"All right, tell me," she whispered. "Did it happen again?"

"You mean the dream?" I shivered, remembering it. Gabby was the only person I'd told about the nightmare that kept coming back. "Of course."

The elevator's oak-paneled doors slid open and we walked into the lobby. "I wish I could just figure out what it *means*," I added as we waved to my doorman, James, and stepped out into the cool October drizzle.

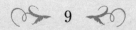

Gabby tapped one finger against her bottom lip, looking thoughtful. Both her parents are psychologists, so Gabby and her little brother, Carlos, are always overanalyzing everything. "Maybe the nightmare represents your worries," she mused.

"Worries about what?" I asked. I tilted back my head to gaze up at the gargoyles that jutted out from the top of my apartment building. The hideous, gnarled stone faces dripped with rain. When I was younger, I liked to pretend that my building was actually a big, rambling haunted house, smack in the middle of the Upper West Side. Sometimes I still liked to imagine it, especially on a gray day like today.

"Student council," Gabby answered swiftly, opening her umbrella. "You're nervous about today's meeting."

"I don't need a dream to tell me *that*." I sighed, linking arms with Gabby and huddling under her umbrella as we walked north along Central Park West. People zipped by us on their way to the subway, sipping coffee and talking into their cell phones. "But if you're right," I added, "it's all your fault."

Back in September, Gabby had declared that we should both sign up for an after-school activity

because it would look good on our college appli-
cations. When I'd reminded Gabby that we were
in the *seventh grade* — and that she already took
ballet, and I took an art and drawing class — she'd
given me one of her Practical Looks and told me to
just trust her.

So that was how I'd been strong-armed into join-
ing student council, which meets Monday and
Thursday afternoons. So far it's been pretty awful.
The one good thing about it is that Gabby and I can
use the meetings as catch-up time, because our only
period together this semester is lunch. And at least
today's meeting would be about the upcoming
Halloween dance, which was something I was actually interested in. Halloween is my favorite holiday.
It's the one time of year when everyone else is as
into dark, spooky stuff as I am.

"I'm sorry, Em," Gabby said brightly as we crossed
86th Street. "But you can't hide in your room *all* the
time, avoiding the world and sketching."

Why not? I thought sourly as our school, West
Side Preparatory, came into view up ahead. Those
things sounded way better than *any* extracurricular
activity.

Maybe Gabby didn't get me so well after all.

Chapter Two

"Order! Order!"

Ashlee Lambert, student council president, banged her pink sparkly gavel on the desk.

Yes. A pink sparkly gavel. Ashlee's mom, who is a judge, had it specially made for her precious daughter. And Ashlee clearly couldn't get enough of the thing.

Bang. Bang.

"This meeting will now come to order!" Ashlee squealed in her high-pitched voice. "We have important business to take care of."

"Item one," I muttered to Gabby. "Steal the pink gavel and bury it somewhere."

Gabby put her hand over her mouth to muffle her laughter. It was three thirty, and we were sitting in the back of Classroom 101, the headquarters of the junior high student council. West Side Prep is divided up into three sections: elementary, junior high, and high school. The junior high student council is traditionally run by an eighth grader. But there was no doubt this year that Ashlee would be our fearless leader, even though she's a seventh grader like me. And since the president gets to pick the cabinet, all of Ashlee's buddies were in power positions, too.

Gag.

At the moment, Ashlee was standing in front of the blackboard, trying to get the attention of the fifteen other kids, who were talking, texting, and otherwise recovering from a grueling Monday. Our teacher-advisor, Ms. Goldsmith, was sitting on the windowsill, reading the *New York Times* and occasionally glancing out at the pouring rain, as if she wanted to escape. I could relate.

Ms. Goldsmith is the social studies teacher, and she's young and pretty, with light brown hair and a soft, sweet voice. In that morning's class, she had assigned us our big project for the semester: a genealogy paper about our family histories. As my friend Padma and I agreed afterward, Ms. Goldsmith somehow made the whole thing sound fun. She's always energetic in class, but by the time student council rolls around, she seems exhausted and pretty much lets Ashlee run the show.

"Time to take attendance!" Ashlee announced as people began to quiet down. She tossed her shiny, white-blond hair over one shoulder and batted her long lashes. "Henry, would you do the honors?"

Henry Green, vice president, stood up and took the clipboard Ashlee handed him. When he faced the classroom, I felt my cheeks get the tiniest bit hot.

Gabby snuck me a knowing smile, then leaned over and scribbled in the margin of my notebook: *Admit it.* I bit my lip and wrote back, pressing hard on the paper: Never.

"It" was the crush Gabby was certain I had on Henry Green. And okay, yes, maybe Henry is kind of cute. He's the tallest boy in our grade, and he has wavy dark hair and light green eyes that always seem to sparkle. *But* he's also captain of the boys' soccer team, and a member of Ashlee's popular crowd. Any boy I'd bother to have a crush on would never be any of those things. The boy I'd have a crush on would listen to punk music, wear all black, and collect spiders. And maybe, just maybe, he'd look a little like Henry Green. I hadn't met this boy yet.

Gabby started to write something back, but then Henry called, "Gabrielle Marquez?" and she jerked her head up.

"Here!" she called, smiling.

Gabby freely admits that she thinks Henry is cute and smart — they're in Ms. Goldsmith's fifth period social studies together, and she says Henry always gets A's on his tests. But Gabby's real crush is Milo, a boy in her ballet class. She's sure any boy brave enough to take ballet has got to be cool (but she and Milo haven't spoken yet).

Henry glanced back down at the alphabetical list. The corner of his mouth turned up slightly. "Pale Paley?" he called out.

I bristled. That's the other thing about Henry. He thinks it's so-o funny that my last name is Paley, and my skin is pale. Whenever I pass him in the hallway, he'll smirk at me and make that same joke. Which is another reason I'd never actually like him.

"Here," I said, glancing down at my desk. "And it's, um, it's Emma-Rose."

"Yes, please stick to real names, Henry,"

Ms. Goldsmith spoke, looking up from her newspaper.

When Henry was finished with attendance, Ashlee wrote: Halloween Dance!! across the blackboard, her charm bracelet jangling.

"All right, everyone," she said, straightening the white belt she wore around her peach-colored dress. (My mother would have definitely approved of Ashlee's all-pastel-all-the-time wardrobe.) "First off, the date of the dance has been moved up one day to accommodate the high school's dance schedule. Our dance is now taking place *on* Halloween — Friday, October thirty-first. That means we have less than two weeks to arrange everything."

Groans echoed throughout the classroom. My stomach sank, and Gabby and I exchanged disappointed glances. Mom's opening gala at the museum was on Halloween! Plus, Gabby and I had been planning on trick-or-treating in my apartment building before I left for the party. We knew we were getting a little old for it, but our yearly tradition was too much fun to give up.

"So the high school gets to have *their* dance on Saturday?" cried Zora Robinson, a friendly eighth grader who wore her dark hair in pretty cornrows.

"Total injustice!" said Roger Chang, student council secretary, Henry's best friend, and captain of the basketball team.

"What about trick-or-treating?" asked Eve Epstein — student council treasurer, Ashlee's best friend, and my number one tormentor in gym class. Ashlee leveled Eve with a look, and then responded in a tone so icy it made the hairs on the back of my neck stand up.

"Seriously, Eve? Don't tell me you *still* go trick-or-treating?"

Silence.

"Oh. Uh." Eve laughed nervously, fiddling with her charm bracelet; it was identical to Ashlee's. "No. Of course not! I was just kidding!" Her face bright red, she stared down at her patent leather ballet flats — which were also identical to Ashlee's.

Princess Ashlee keeps her subjects in check! Gabby wrote in my notebook. In response I drew a quick sketch of Eve with X's in place of her eyes, and her tongue hanging out of her mouth. Gabby giggled.

"But the dance doesn't start until seven o'clock," Henry spoke up, sticking his hands in the back pockets of his jeans. "So, for those of you who, you know, *might* want to go trick-or-treating beforehand, you'd have time." He ducked his head, smiling. I hated that I thought he had a nice smile.

Ashlee rolled her baby-blue eyes. But when Henry glanced at her, she pasted on a fake grin and changed the subject to the school's new recycling program. Meanwhile, Gabby wrote me another note: *Whew! Candy, here we come!*

I nodded, but I didn't have the heart to write back. I was glad that trick-or-treating was still on. But Mom's gala, like the dance, was scheduled to begin at seven o'clock.

I'd been looking forward to the gala so much. I even had my outfit picked out: a short, black satin skirt with a tulle hem, and a ruffle-front purple top. There were supposed to be fancy hors d'oeuvres, live music, and famous people — at the last gala, Mom had met the mayor and at least four movie stars.

At the same time, though, I couldn't miss the dance. I knew Gabby, Padma, and Caitlin really wanted to go, and, despite my issues with Ashlee and her crew, I wanted to be there, too. It would be so fun dressing up in costume — I was deciding between a Goth ghost or Hermione, or possibly a Goth Hermione — and dancing with my friends.

So what am I going to do? I wondered, chewing on the end of my pen. Gala or dance? I couldn't attend both. Somehow, I'd have to choose.

An hour later, I arrived home, eager to discuss my Halloween problem with Dad. I hadn't been able to talk to Gabby because her mom had picked her up from the meeting to take her to the dentist. But I hoped Dad would give me good advice.

As I dropped my soggy umbrella in the foyer, I heard voices and laughter coming from the living room. That was odd. Dad was usually still in his study at this time, and Mom didn't get home from work until six o'clock. I took off my backpack, shook out my rain-damp hair, and headed down the shadowy hallway. I passed Bram, who was asleep on his big pillow, then turned into the living room. What I found there made me gasp.

Mom and Dad were sitting on the sofa with the strangest-looking woman I had ever seen. She had white-white skin, ruby red lips, and black hair piled up on her head in an elaborate bun. She wore a velvet choker with a glittery black butterfly pendant, and her flowing black dress was printed with bold slashes of red. Her long nails were painted crimson, and black eyeliner made her eyes look big and dramatic.

The woman glanced over at me, and her whole face lit up.

"Emma-Rose! My dah-link!" she exclaimed in a heavy accent. She rose so gracefully from the sofa she seemed to be floating. "At last, ve meet."

"Um," I said, glancing at Mom and Dad for help. I wanted to ask the woman, *Who are you?* but I thought that might seem kind of rude.

"Come on, honey," Mom said, waving me forward. "Give your great-aunt Margo a hug."

I was so shocked I could barely move. *This* was Great-aunt Margo? She looked nothing like my grandmother, her sister. Grandma, from what I remembered, had been silver-haired and wrinkly, with Mom's twinkling gray eyes. Great-aunt Margo's face was smooth and ageless, and her eyes were a deep, almost navy, blue.

But as she approached me and spread her arms wide, I realized something. A chill raced down my spine.

Great-aunt Margo looked like . . . *me.*

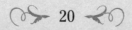

An older — and sort of beautiful — version of me, to be sure. But there was a very strong resemblance. *Does she see it, too?* I wondered as she wrapped me in a big hug. She was surprisingly strong, and practically squeezed the breath out of me. Her cheek, pressed against mine, was cold, but the embrace itself felt warm and inviting. She smelled like rich, flowery perfume.

As Great-aunt Margo drew back, my eyes landed on her butterfly choker. Up close, I could see that the pendant was not a butterfly after all. The black wings were long and had a familiar crooked shape.

"It's . . . it's a bat!" I exclaimed, then immediately felt silly. *Those* were my first words to my great-aunt? Pure brilliance. "I mean — it's really cool," I added honestly, gazing at the tiny, bejeweled creature. The pendant was totally something I would have bought for myself.

A slow smile spread across Margo's face. Her teeth were very white against her red lips. "You like it, dah-link?" she said. "Then you must see my collection."

"Oh, are you a jewelry designer?" I asked eagerly. I'd always assumed my artistic abilities came from

Dad, but maybe I'd inherited them from Great-aunt Margo.

"No, Margo is a biologist," Mom interrupted, standing up and walking over to us. I felt a wave of disappointment. It seemed like Great-aunt Margo would have a much more glamorous job. "A famous one, in fact," Mom added. "She's Romania's leading expert on the *Desmodus rotundus*."

"What's that?" I asked, wishing I paid better attention in science class.

Great-aunt Margo smiled again. "The common vampire bat."

Goose bumps broke out on my arms. "Aren't those . . . aren't those the kind that suck people's blood?" I heard my voice turn a little shaky. I remembered catching a glimpse of some Discovery Channel special last Halloween.

"Yeah, but don't worry," Dad laughed, getting to his feet. "The ones Margo brought over here have been dead for a long time."

"Here?" I echoed, glancing around the living room. There were bats in our apartment? I was grossed out, but also kind of fascinated.

"They're in the guest room," Dad explained, smiling at my expression. "Margo is also an expert on taxidermy — the art of treating and stuffing a dead animal's skin to make it look alive again."

"Like in the museum?" I asked, thinking of the stuffed bears, wolves, and deer that were displayed at the Museum of Natural History. I'd grown up visiting those animals, but never really thought about the fact that they weren't statues. They'd once been *alive*.

"Exactly," Mom put in. "That's Margo's contribution to the Creatures of the Night exhibit — she's providing us with the world's largest collection of stuffed bats."

So *that* was what Margo had meant by her "collection." I felt my heart start to thump. The guest room was next door to my bedroom. Maybe I would peek inside later.

Maybe.

Great-aunt Margo raised one dark eyebrow at me, as if she could read my thoughts. I glanced away from her quickly. I imagined the IM I'd send Gabby later: *My great-aunt is a little weird. Even weirder than me!*

"Okay, enough work talk," Mom said, clapping her hands. "Who's hungry?"

"I was planning to grill some burgers," Dad said

as Mom ushered us out of the living room. "Sound good to everyone?"

"Can you actually make mine a veggie burger, hon?" Mom asked. She must have been inspired by Gabby.

"And please make mine rare?" I requested.

Dad smiled at me and said, "As always."

"Yes, I prefer rare as vell," Great-aunt Margo said, resting a delicate hand on her stomach. "It vill be lovely to eat a real meal. Airplane cuisine leaves much to be desired."

We all walked down the hall toward the dining room, where a big salad bowl was already on the table, along with four place settings. As we passed Bram on his pillow, he jolted awake, his ears pricking up and his back arching.

"He must have heard the word *burgers*," Dad chuckled, reaching down to give our dog a pat. I watched Bram, sensing something strange about him.

Bram looked at Great-aunt Margo and growled softly. Then he opened his mouth, threw back his head, and let out an ear-piercing howl. I had never heard Bram — or any dog — make that kind of sound. Before Dad could stop him, Bram hopped off his pillow and scrambled down the hall, his nails click-clicking on the floor.

"What on earth?" Dad gasped. He stared after Bram, who'd practically left a cloud of dust in his wake.

"Wow!" I exclaimed, looking at my great-aunt. "I think Bram just found someone he likes even less than me!"

"Emma-Rose!" Mom admonished me.

But Great-aunt Margo was laughing, and she reached out to squeeze my hand. Her fingers, like her cheek, were cold, but once again her gesture made me feel warm and secure. "You are right, my dah-link," she chuckled. "Vhat can I say? Canines and I have never gotten along."

"Same here," I laughed as she and I settled down at the table. Dad went into the kitchen to start grilling, and Mom peered at the salad.

"Hon?" she called to Dad. "Which dressing did you use?"

"The Italian one," Dad called back. "Why?"

Mom sighed, lifting up the bowl and carrying it toward the kitchen. "We can't serve this then," she told Dad. "Margo's allergic to garlic."

"You *are*?" I asked my great-aunt, jealous. "Ugh, I

hate garlic! I wish I was allergic. Then Mom would stop trying to make me eat it!"

"Garlic is very healthy!" Mom called from the kitchen.

Great-aunt Margo leaned across the table, shooting me a mischievous smile. "Healthy, but disgusting, no?" she whispered, and I grinned at her.

For the first time in my life, I felt like someone in my family finally understood me. And I was really glad that Great-aunt Margo had come to visit.

Even if she was a little weird.

Chapter Three

Over a delicious dinner of perfectly cooked hamburgers, Great-aunt Margo talked about her hometown in Romania. A small village with a funny name, it was nestled deep in the Carpathian Mountains, and it sounded beautiful. Margo described lush green forests, clear blue streams, narrow cobblestone streets, and ancient castles.

As she spoke — and Mom chimed in with memories of photographs her parents had shown her — I glanced out the window at the Manhattan skyline. Though I loved the tall buildings and concrete sidewalks of New York City, I liked the idea of such a rural, quaint place . . . the place my ancestors had lived! Suddenly, I realized that Great-aunt Margo had given me a great starting point for my social studies project.

Excited, I helped with the dishes and excused myself for the night. Then I headed into my room, grabbed my laptop, and sat cross-legged on my bed.

I opened Google, then typed in the name of my family's Romanian village, grateful for the *Did you mean?* feature after I'd misspelled it twice. Then I clicked on the Wikipedia page; it showed a pretty picture of the forests Great-aunt Margo had talked about, and gave the basic facts: population, map coordinates, and weather. Then, as I skimmed the page, I spotted a sentence that made my jaw drop.

Located in the region once known as Transylvania, this small town is still home to many vampire legends.

I sat back, my pulse racing. *Transylvania?* As in, Count Dracula territory? I had no idea that my family came from *there*. Intrigued, I started to read more, but then my IM pinged. It was Gabby.

Bad news! she'd written. Dentist said I have to get braces! ☹

I was still preoccupied by the whole Transylvania thing, but I tried to turn my attention to my best friend.

That totally bites! I typed back, hoping to make her smile.

Her response popped up immediately: Am so not LOL-ing. Of course u can joke about it, Em. U have perfect teeth!

I shook my head. Though my dentist had recently declared that I wouldn't need braces (I'd celebrated with a candy feast that had resulted in three cavities), my teeth were *far* from perfect. I rose up on my knees so I was facing the mirror above my dresser, and I opened my mouth in an exaggerated smile. There they were, in the corners of my mouth — my super-embarrassing, super-pointy teeth. My dentist called them "incisors" and had even remarked that mine were sharper than most. I knew he was being nice by not calling them what they really were: fangs.

I heard another *ping!* and glanced back at my computer.

And ur "fangs" don't count! Gabby had written.

She seemed upset, so I decided to call her. We chatted for a while, discussing Great-aunt Margo ("definitely weird," Gabby said), my dance vs. gala issue ("definitely dance," Gabby declared), and braces ("get colored ones and make them a fashion statement," I advised). By the time we said good-bye, it was late, so I finished the Edgar Allan Poe story I had to read for English, brushed my imperfect teeth, changed into my pj's, and crawled into bed.

But, of course, I couldn't sleep.

First, I flipped onto my side, then my belly, then my back. Passing headlights from cars threw strange shapes onto my ceiling. The falling raindrops sounded like fingertips tapping against my windowpane. I thought about Edgar Allan Poe, Halloween, Henry Green (for just a second), Great-aunt Margo, and the genealogy project. Then I remembered the Wikipedia page I'd stopped reading, and I sat up.

Without turning on the light, I eased out of bed and walked over to my desk. Sinking into my chair, I opened my laptop, and went back to where I had left off:

Located in the region once known as Transylvania, this small town is still home to many vampire legends. One such legend is about a certain breed of vampires who can shape-shift into bats, which then feast upon human and animal blood. In ancient times, villagers became so fearful that they hung knobs of garlic from their doorways, as it was said that the scent warded off the fanged creatures.

BANG!

The loud sound made me jump up so fast that I almost knocked over my chair. The bang hadn't been a clap of thunder, or one of the many sirens I was used to hearing at all hours. It hadn't even come from outside. It had come from right next door.

From the guest room.

Maybe Great-aunt Margo, like me, had trouble sleeping. Maybe she was unpacking, and the two of us could have a midnight snack. Maybe we could even discuss the vampire legends of her town. I was curious to learn more. For someone who enjoyed horror stories, I knew very little about vampires.

I tiptoed into the hallway. A window was open somewhere in the apartment, and I shivered in my thin pajamas. As my eyes adjusted to the darkness, I saw that Bram was back on his pillow, fast asleep, and that the door to my parents' bedroom was closed. But the door to the guest room was ajar.

Moving as silently as possible, I crept over and paused on the threshold. The long, narrow room was blanketed in darkness, and the one window at its far end was open. The damp breeze lifted the gauzy white curtains, making them dance like restless ghosts. Piles of fancy-looking luggage were in the center of the room, and the scent of Great-aunt Margo's perfume filled the air. But Margo herself was nowhere to be found. The bed was still neatly made, and the room was empty.

Except for the cages and cages full of bats.

Stuffed bats, I reminded myself as I stepped inside. I held my breath, spooked by the sight of the dark, silent creatures. They all hung upside down from the bars of the cages, their leathery wings tucked against their furry bodies and their beady eyes shut tight. *Like they're sleeping*, I thought, shuddering.

Great-aunt Margo was even weirder than I'd thought! Did she put her stuffed bats into these poses every night, as if they were her dolls or pets or something? And where *was* she? She couldn't have gone outside in the rain. Was she in the kitchen?

Before I could turn to leave the room, lightning flashed outside, and I gave a start. For a second, the bat cage nearest me was lit up, and I saw that the cage door was swinging wide open. That must have been the bang I'd heard earlier: the wind blowing open the cage. I leaned over to close the small door.

Suddenly, one of the bats inside opened its eyes.

Its tiny, bright red eyes.

My knees turned to jelly, and I tripped backward. Before I could think, I dashed out of the room and into the hall, pressing my back against the wall and breathing hard.

Calm down, Emma-Rose.

I thought about what practical Gabby would say if she were there. *It's just your overactive imagination*, she'd tell me, chuckling. She'd probably say that the moonlight had been playing tricks on me. That my mind was still full of the vampires and bats I'd been reading about on the Internet. That I should go back to bed, because there was absolutely no way that any of those bats were alive.

But then why were they in cages?

My curiosity took hold of me and didn't let go.

Sliding my back along the wall, I turned my head and peeked into the guest room, not wanting to go inside again.

My heart stopped.

A glossy black bat with long, graceful wings flew in through the open window and balanced on the sill. The bat's eyes were trained on the other bats in their cages. Like clockwork, all the bats in the room began unfolding their wings and opening their eyes, waking up. They even yawned, revealing pointy fangs.

And then —

The bat on the windowsill began to transform. The wings disappeared and were replaced by long, graceful arms. The squat, furry body lengthened out and began to take on a human form. As I stared, my eyes growing wider, my pulse pounding at my throat, the big bat ears shrunk. Then the tiny bat head began to morph into a human face. A *familiar* human face.

The face of Great-aunt Margo.

I clapped my hand over my mouth to silence my scream. All I wanted to do was run, but my legs wouldn't work.

Please let this be one of those nightmares, I prayed over and over. *Please let Mom call my name. Please let me wake up in my bed.*

But I didn't wake up. I stood there, trembling from head to toe, and staring at my great-aunt, who was no longer a bat. She now stood regally in front of the window, still watching the cages. She looked exactly as she had earlier that night, in her flowing black dress, with her hair in its bun. Only this time, the dark red lipstick on her mouth almost looked as if it could be — blood.

What should I do? I wondered wildly. *Yell for help? Wake up Mom and Dad?* Even if I'd wanted to, my throat had gone bone-dry.

Slowly, Great-aunt Margo turned her gaze away from the bats, and in one choking second of terror, I realized she was about to see me. Finally, I was able to move. I spun around and tore toward my bedroom. With quivering hands, I shut the door. Then I flung myself onto my bed, burrowing under my covers and trying to stop my teeth from chattering.

Did I really see that? Did she see me? Am I going crazy? Is she about to knock on my door? My mind was racing as fast as my heart.

After I'd pinched myself — hard — to make sure I really *was* awake, and I'd waited a good while to make sure Great-aunt Margo wasn't coming after me, I lifted my head out from under the covers. The apartment was as silent as it had been before the fateful bang. There were no voices, and no sounds of flapping wings. If I strained my ears, all I could hear were Dad's snores.

What was going on inside the guest room? Had the other bats also transformed into people? Or had they all flown out into the night?

On my desk, my laptop screen was still bright. The whole horrifying experience had happened so quickly that my computer hadn't even gone to sleep. I knew *I* wouldn't be sleeping much that night. But I couldn't bring myself to get out of bed and go back to reading the Wikipedia page. Besides, I wasn't sure I needed to. I remembered almost every sentence, and the words drummed through my head now.

The fanged creatures. Knobs of garlic. Vampires who can shape-shift into bats.

Vampires who could shape-shift into bats . . . who came from the very town that Great-aunt Margo came from. Great-aunt Margo, who was "allergic" to garlic.

I drew my knees to my chest and sat still in the darkness while the storm raged outside. All my life, I'd suspected that there were secrets lurking behind the ordinary, that there was more to reality than met the eye. And now, I had actual evidence.

The realization struck me all at once, as fast as a flash of lightning. It was so crazy, but so obvious that I couldn't deny it.

My great-aunt was a lot more than just weird.

She was a vampire.

Chapter Four

"What's wrong, honey?"

Sunlight flooded my room, and Mom leaned over my bed, her eyes concerned. I was lying on my back, clutching my sketchbook to my chest. Last night, I'd started drawing to calm down, and must have somehow fallen asleep. Now, my hair was sweaty and matted, and I could barely lift my heavy eyelids. I understood why Mom looked worried; this was much worse than my usual morning grouchiness.

What's wrong? I thought. *Well, you see, Mom, I think Great-aunt Margo is a vampire, so we should all start wearing turtlenecks. Oh, and we should hang garlic everywhere.*

But I was too drained to even respond.

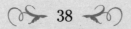

"I've never seen you so pale," Mom said, touching my forehead. "Maybe you're coming down with a cold. Do you want to stay home from school?"

Normally, those words would have made me grin and snuggle deeper into bed, especially on such a sun-splashed day. But now, Mom's suggestion only filled me with dread. I was *not* about to stay cooped up with vampire bats. I had seen far too much last night to feel safe in my own home.

And I had to warn Mom and Dad.

I tried to lift my head from the pillow. "Great-aunt Margo —" I began, feeling a shudder pass through me as I spoke her name.

"Oh, she's not here, hon," Mom said, and I felt a wave of relief. Maybe she'd flown (literally flown) back to Romania.

"She left very early, before sunrise, to take her bats to the museum," Mom continued. "I'm supposed to meet her there soon, but I can go in later if you want. Dad has a deadline, so he's going to be in the study all day."

Panic rose up in me. "Mom, don't — don't go to the museum," I gasped. "Not because of me — because of the bats. They're real. They're dangerous. Actually, you should call the museum and tell them. . . ." I struggled to sit up, and my sketchbook slid off me and clattered to the floor.

Mom knelt down to pick up my sketchbook. She glanced at the illustration I'd begun in the middle of the night: a woman with the head and wings of a bat. I couldn't help it; I'd had to sketch what I'd witnessed. Drawing is what helps me make sense of things, even things that make zero sense.

"See?" I said desperately, pointing to the sketch. "I went into Great-aunt Margo's room last night, and I saw something really scary."

"Emma-Rose." Mom sighed, setting my sketchbook on the bedside table. She frowned at my skull wallpaper and the Edgar Allan Poe book on my desk. "I know you have a taste for all things dark and macabre. And since Margo is a little eccentric, it's fun for you to invent stories. But you've made yourself sick by staying up late and drawing!"

Fun? Was she kidding?

"Mom, I'm not sick!" I cried. I felt a rush of frustration. "And I'm not making anything up. Great-aunt Margo is a —"

"I remember when you were little," Mom interrupted, smiling down at me fondly. "You used to tell me our building was haunted! It was so cute."

I rolled my eyes. I should have known Mom wouldn't believe me. Then I had a thought. Maybe Mom already *knew* the truth about Great-aunt Margo. Mom was her niece, after all. Maybe Grandma had even told Mom about Margo's secret identity, years ago, and Mom was acting this way as a cover-up.

But when I searched my mother's face, her expression remained the same: amused and a little worried. But not worried that I now knew some deep, dark family secret — just worried that her daughter had gone off the deep end.

Besides, I thought, as Mom took my shoulders and gently laid me back down, if my mother knew what Great-aunt Margo really was, she wouldn't have subjected me and Dad to such possible danger, would she?

And why didn't *Great-aunt Margo try to bite any of us last night?* I wondered. Was there some vampire code about whom you could and couldn't attack?

I was so distracted by these thoughts that I forgot to protest as Mom covered me with my blanket. "You need to rest," she was saying. "I'll phone the school to tell them you're sick today. Dad will be here, but call me at work if you need anything."

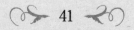

No, you call ME *if Great-aunt Margo's bats come to life and start sucking the blood of the museum staff!*

As Mom left, I wanted to yell after her that I was fine. Part of me was dying to walk to school with Gabby and have a perfectly ordinary day. But, at the same time, *ordinary* no longer seemed to be an option. How could I get through classes like social studies and gym while worrying about fangs and blood? So I staggered out of bed and texted Gabby that I was "under the weather." I figured I could tell my best friend the terrifying truth once the school day was over.

Walking out of my room, I took a breath and glanced into the guest room: the scene of the crime. The bat cages were gone, and Great-aunt Margo's luggage was stashed in a corner. The bright, sunny room couldn't have looked more innocent. For a second, I wondered if I *had* imagined, or dreamed, all the horrors of last night.

In the kitchen, Dad had prepared me a steaming mug of tea and two pieces of toast. He seemed stressed about his deadline, so I knew better than to try to convince *him* about Great-aunt Margo. I did suggest that he serve garlic for dinner that night, which only made him give me a strange glance and touch my forehead, like Mom had. Then he took Bram out for a walk, leaving me alone in the kitchen with just the TV for company.

As always, Dad had been watching New York 1. I took a sip of tea, distractedly glancing at the screen. Then I did a double take. The news reporter was standing on the corner of Central Park West and 86th Street — right in our neighborhood. Maybe I'd see Dad and Bram in the background.

The reporter looked very serious. "Residents of the Upper West Side are alarmed by a disturbing discovery made by a jogger earlier this morning," she said. "The dead bodies of several squirrels and raccoons were found in Central Park, not far from the 86th Street Transverse. The animals all displayed the same bizarre, two-pronged bite marks on their necks, prompting some residents to wonder if a wild animal might have escaped from the Central Park Zoo."

My mug began to shake in my hand, and some scalding tea sloshed over the side. I barely noticed.

An elderly woman I recognized from my apartment building appeared on-screen. "I remember that something like this happened thirteen years ago," she said in a gravelly voice. "Nobody caught the predator then, but I hope they catch it now."

Next the camera went to a hot-dog vendor. "It's definitely scary," he said. "Sounds like the work of a hawk. Or it could be a cougar."

Or, I thought, chills tiptoeing down my neck, *a vampire.*

Many vampires, to be exact. Vampire bats. I pictured them — a great black flock, flying out of our apartment, past the gargoyles, and into the darkness of the park.

"Residents are advised to avoid the park at night, if possible," the reporter said. "We will keep you posted as events unfold."

The weather forecast came on, and I sat on the edge of the chair, my heart hammering. It was too much of a coincidence — the location, the timing, the bite marks. Great-aunt Margo and her "stuffed" bats had to have been behind the attacks.

But at the same time I didn't want to believe it. Yes, I'd seen her in bat form, but I still couldn't picture my great-aunt — with her inviting smile and warm embrace — sucking the blood of innocent creatures. What *else* was she capable of? I wondered with a shiver. And was there any way to stop her and her vampire friends without causing a mass panic in the streets of New York?

I had to learn more.

I set down my mug, my fear and confusion suddenly replaced by determination. Since I was home from school today anyway, I could use the extra time to do research on vampires. That way, I'd have more information if I talked to my parents or — *gulp* — confronted my great-aunt.

Dad and Bram walked in then, and Dad made no mention of seeing news reporters outside. Instead, he went to his study, and Bram curled up on his pillow, glaring at me. It was the perfect opportunity to slip into my room and get to work.

First, I pulled down my window shade, blocking out the sunlight. Then I sat at my desk and woke my sleeping laptop. My heart jumped as the Wikipedia page reappeared. I skimmed it, but there was nothing new beyond what I'd read last night. So I tried something else: I typed the name of my family's village along with the word *vampires* into Google.

I gasped. The search returned almost one *million* results! Some sites, I saw, just repeated the Wikipedia entry, while others mentioned that Count

Dracula himself had passed through the town. Then I spotted a link called "An Introduction to Transylvanian Vampires." It sounded promising, so I clicked through.

The page was black with red type, and had an old-fashioned illustration of a man in a black cape, baring his fangs and leaning over a fainting woman. Underneath the drawing was a list, simply titled "Common Traits of Vampires":

- *Aversion to sunlight.*
- *Nocturnal, hunting only by night.*
- *Fair skin that is cold to the touch.*
- *Inability to appear in mirrors, or in photographs.*
- *Inability to grow older past a certain age. Also, immortality.*
- *Appetite for blood and rare meat.*
- *Superhuman strength.*
- *Tendency to frighten domesticated animals, such as dogs or cats.*
- *Ability to shape-shift into bats.*

I nodded, overwhelmed. That last item had the biggest "check" next to it. Great-aunt Margo was precisely what I'd thought she was.

True, I had no evidence — yet — that she didn't show up in mirrors or photographs. Or that she was immortal. But she definitely had pale, cool skin. Judging by the hug she'd given me yesterday, she was pretty strong. She'd definitely frightened Bram, and she *had* requested her burger rare.

Wait.

I paused, my fingers freezing on the keyboard. A cold sensation began to spread through my stomach.

Great-aunt Margo ate her burgers rare, and she was pale, and Bram hated her. . . .

Just . . . like . . . me.

The cold feeling traveled to my limbs. I gasped for air, trying to calm myself. Then I read the list again, from the beginning, focusing on every detail.

I knew the word *aversion*; it had been on our English vocabulary quiz the week before. It meant a dislike of something. Such as my dislike of sunshine. *Sunlight* and *sunshine* were pretty much the same thing. And I had an aversion to them, didn't I?

That fits, sang a small voice in my head.

I held my breath as I moved down the list. *Nocturnal.* Another big word, but the list explained its meaning; it had to do with nighttime.

Nighttime, when I felt most awake, when my thoughts were sharp and my senses alert. Almost as if I were ready to . . .

Hunt.

No.

Tiny shivers were crawling up and down my arms like spiders. What was wrong with me? What was I even thinking? I needed to stay on track: I was supposed to be researching vampires. Great-aunt Margo. This had nothing to do with me.

I scrolled down past the list, and came to the paragraph at the bottom of the page. I read it hungrily:

The region of the Carpathian mountains historically called Transylvania — literally meaning "on the other side of the forest" — has long been home to large, sprawling vampire dynasties. Legend has it that young boys and girls of these ancient families begin showing the above traits at the age of twelve, and become full-fledged vampires shortly thereafter. It is also believed that vampirism is passed down along the maternal line, and can sometimes skip generations.

I stared at the screen so hard my eyes burned. The word *maternal* had also been on our vocab quiz last week. It meant *motherly*, as in, the mother's side of the family.

As in Great-aunt Margo, my mom's aunt.

Which meant . . .

My pulse began to race.

My grandmother couldn't have been a vampire. She was dead, and if vampires didn't age and lived forever . . . well, then, that ruled her out. As for Mom, there was no way she was a vampire. Mom liked veggie burgers and sunshine. She slept easily at night. Bram liked her. And she was . . . *Mom*.

Which left only one person to consider.

I swallowed hard.

Me.

Dizzy, I jumped up and glanced at myself in the mirror. There I was, in my rumpled pj's, with my dark hair in a sloppy bun. My face was as pale as a phantom's, and my navy blue eyes — so similar to Great-aunt Margo's — were wide with terror.

See, you have a reflection! I told myself. But then I opened my mouth, wider and wider, until I could see my sharp incisors.

That fits, too.

I was like Great-aunt Margo in so many ways. I had trouble sleeping. I had fangs. I had practically every trait on that list.

My heart was pounding hard enough to burst out of my chest.

Is that why I am the way I am? I wondered.

I looked around my darkened room. Everything seemed so normal: my messy bed, my sketch pad with the drawings of the bat-woman, my purple curtains, my bookshelf. But nothing was truly normal anymore.

Last night, the Great-aunt Margo discovery had thrown me for a loop. But this was something much bigger. Something I couldn't have thought of in a million years.

Chapter Five

"I'm a vampire."

Gabby held open the door to her brownstone, her jaw slack as she stared at me.

I repeated my confession, lifting my chin and trying to keep my voice even.

"I'm a vampire," I said.

Gabby stared at me for a moment longer, her brown eyes round. Then, slowly, her face broke into a smile.

"That's such a good idea!" she laughed, bouncing up and down in her Converse sneakers. "A vampire! Why didn't we think of that before? You've got the skin tone, you just need to smear fake blood around your mouth, and get those plastic fangs, and you'll have the best Halloween costume ever. . . ."

She trailed off when she noticed that I wasn't laughing. Or speaking. I just stood on her stoop, wearing my big sunglasses and holding my duffel bag.

Back in my room, I'd realized two things: that I couldn't face Great-aunt Margo that night — what if she knew what I was and wanted me to go hunting with her? — and that I had to talk to Gabby ASAP.

It had been torture waiting for the time to pass, but as soon as my bedside clock struck two thirty, I'd sprung into action. I'd yanked on my jeans, black flats, and gray hoodie, and thrown a bunch of stuff into my duffel bag. Then I'd knocked on the door to Dad's study and asked for permission to stay at Gabby's house that night. Luckily, Dad was too distracted by his deadline to ask any questions. He only told me to call him and Mom later to check in.

"Em, are you still feeling sick?" Gabby asked, peering at me with the same worried expression Mom and Dad had worn that morning. She took my arm and pulled me into her house. "We missed you at school today. Do you have the flu or something?"

I shook my head. "I *am* sick," I whispered, removing my sunglasses with trembling hands, "but not in the way you think."

Gabby raised her eyebrows. "Em, you're kind of scaring me."

You don't know the half of it.

A loud yell from the living room made me press a hand to my chest. "Who's in there?" I hissed, peeking over Gabby's shoulder. I was so panicked that I expected to see a swarm of bats.

"Carlos, of course." Gabby rolled her eyes as she usually did when it came to her younger brother. "He's, like, surgically attached to his Wii. Especially when my parents are at work. You'd think he'd let us play *one* —"

"We need to talk," I interrupted. "In private."

"O-kay," Gabby said, still looking at me like I'd sprouted an extra head. She led me past an oblivious Carlos to her small, apple green bedroom, locking the door. I let out a huge breath and dropped my duffel bag on the floor with a thunk.

"What do you *have* in that thing?" Gabby asked as she moved a plate of banana slices — her annoyingly healthy after-school snack — off her bed. "A dead body?"

Which was absolutely the worst thing to say.

I burst into tears.

"Oh no! Em!" Gabby cried, rushing over and giving me a hug. "What's the *matter*? Please tell me. You're freaking me out."

"If — if this — is freaking you out," I sob-hiccuped into Gabby's shoulder, "then — then you don't want to know what — what's really going on."

"Shh. Okay. Chill out," Gabby said soothingly, putting her arm around me and leading me over to the bed. "Whatever it is, it can't be that bad."

"Oh yeah?" I challenged as we sat down. "It's worse than bad. And you *have* to promise not to tell Padma or Caitlin or anyone at school."

Padma and Caitlin are great, but if they knew my scary secret, they'd likely blab about it to their friends on the girls' soccer team. From there, it would spread to all the other sports teams, and trickle into the academic clubs, and before long, all of West Side Prep would get the bulletin:

EMMA-ROSE PALEY: FANGED AND DANGEROUS!

And what if Henry Green found out? My heart lurched at the thought.

Not that I cared.

Right?

"Of course I promise," Gabby said, grabbing the box of tissues off her nightstand.

I swiped at my damp cheeks with my hand. "Okay. Remember what I told you on your stoop just now?"

Gabby handed me a Kleenex. "That you want to be a vampire for Halloween?"

I shook my head. "I don't *want* to be a vampire, Gab. I *am* one." I blew my nose, then looked steadily at my best friend. "A bloodsucker. Dracula. Bats. You know. *That* kind of vampire. Only . . . real."

There. I'd said it.

Gabby bit her bottom lip, then gently tucked a strand of hair behind my ear. "Em, was this another bad dream?" she asked softly.

I shook my head vehemently, twisting the tissue in my hands. "I wish! I know it sounds insane, Gab, but . . ." I exhaled, trying to compose myself. "Okay. I should probably start from the beginning."

So I did. I told Gabby everything. When I got to the part about the bat becoming Great-aunt Margo, Gabby looked skeptical, but she didn't interrupt or question me. And she kept listening as I described the news report and my research on the Internet.

"Don't you see?" I finished, feeling drained. "*It all fits*. Everything fits."

Gabby didn't answer at first. She studied me in her wise way, her tan arms wrapped around her knees. "All right," she said at last, her voice serious and determined. "Let's take this step-by-step."

I nodded eagerly. This was what I relied on Gabby for. She approached everything with a sane, scientific method, while I tended to flail about dramatically. As she stood up and snatched a notepad and pen off her desk, I felt a surge of relief.

"Gab?" I asked as she sat back down. "Does this mean that you . . . believe me?"

"I know you're not lying, Em," Gabby replied, putting on her cute, red-framed glasses. "You have a big imagination, but I don't think it's *that* big."

"Oh, thank you!" I shouted, flinging my arms around my friend. Then, just as quickly, I drew back. "Wait. Do you not want me to hug you? I mean, you're not afraid I might . . . *attack* you?" I whispered. The thought made me shudder.

"Hmm," Gabby said, flipping her notepad to a clean page. "Well, you tell me. Do you *want* to suck my blood?"

I tried to imagine it: my fangs growing longer and coming forward out of my mouth, before sinking into the skin of —

No. No. No. My stomach turned.

"Absolutely not," I replied. "I don't want to suck *anyone's* blood. But especially not yours!"

"Interesting." Gabby made a notation in her pad. "Moving on. You've never, to the best of your knowledge, assumed the shape of a bat, have you?"

"Not that I know of," I said, patting my arms to make sure they were still arms and not shiny black wings. "Unless it happens at night while I'm sleeping or —"

"Doubtful," Gabby interrupted, writing something else down. "We've had enough sleepovers together. I'm sure I would have noticed a *bat* at some point over the years."

"I guess." Maybe I was one of those non-bloodsucking, non-bat-becoming vampires. If there was such a thing.

"And see?" Gabby prompted, pointing to the many photos of me around her room: me and Gabby on a picnic blanket in Central Park; me grinning and holding up my art award from last year; me with Gabby, Padma, Caitlin, and my parents at my birthday dinner over the summer. "You show up in photographs. You don't crave blood. You're not half bat. I don't want to test this one out, but I'm *pretty* sure you're not immortal. Em . . ." Gabby paused, studying her notes before glancing up at me. "The facts speak for themselves. You are not a vampire."

I let her words sink in. Was Gabby *right*? I'd been so certain of my vampire status, but Gabby sounded even more certain. Had I just been jumping to conclusions? It wouldn't have been the first time.

"But what about Bram?" I burst out, throwing up my hands. "Why does he hate me? Why do I love meat so much? And what about the fact that I'm *related* to someone we know *is* a vampire?"

As I was speaking, Gabby was scribbling in her notepad, which was getting on my nerves. I heard the front door unlock and Mr. and Mrs. Marquez come in, greeting Carlos. I hoped Gabby wouldn't share her notes with her psychologist parents. They'd probably recommend I be sent to an institution. Not one for vampires, but for crazy people.

"Okay," Gabby said, sticking her pen behind one ear. "Remember when you got Bram, when we were seven and he was a puppy? And remember how *awful* you were to him? You were always bossing him around, and shrieking every time he had an accident in the apartment. *That's* probably why he doesn't like you."

"Oh." I crumpled the tissue in my fist, surprised at the memory Gabby had brought up. I'd forgotten how hard it had been, adjusting to having a new puppy. "That's a good point."

"As for the meat thing, you probably have an iron deficiency, and need to eat more meat than most people," Gabby continued. "Though you could always just take supplements and switch over to being veggie, like me." She grinned, and I groaned.

"Finally, we *don't* know for a fact that Great-aunt Margo is a vampire," Gabby said. "It sounds like the Central Park attacks were done by a hawk or some-thing. And maybe there's a reasonable explanation for why you saw Margo as a bat. There *are* regular bats that live in Manhattan, you know. Maybe one just flew into Margo's room and in the darkness you got confused. Why don't you just *ask* her?"

I tugged nervously on my hoodie's zipper. *Ask her?* That option hadn't crossed my mind even once during my sleepless night or my frantic day. I pictured myself tapping on the guest room door, and Great-aunt Margo welcoming me in with a warm, "Hello, dah-link!"

What would I say? *Hi, Great-aunt Margo, sorry to bother you, but can you tell me why I saw you in bat form? Oh yeah, and also why all your stuffed bats are actually alive — or possibly undead?*

What if she got angry? What if she . . . bit me?

I reached up to protectively touch my neck.

"I can't," I told Gabby. "I can't ask her. I can't even think about seeing her!" I gestured to my heavy duffel bag by the door. "That's why I dragged that over here. Is it cool if I spend the night?"

"Of course it is," Gabby said, giving me a quick hug. "As long as you promise not to" — she dropped her voice and shot me a wicked grin — "*attack* me."

I couldn't help it; I started laughing and Gabby giggled, too. Suddenly, I realized how silly the whole thing sounded. I wasn't convinced that Great-aunt Margo wasn't a vampire, and I wasn't sure about myself either. But I felt a thousand times better than when I'd first arrived at Gabby's place. Which is why Gabby's the *best* best friend ever.

By then, twilight had started to fall, and a cold breeze wafted into the room. Gabby said she was going to let her parents know I was staying over, and I remembered that I had to call Mom and Dad, too.

Gabby left, and I walked over to my duffel bag to get my cell phone. On my way, my eyes landed on one of the photographs on Gabby's wall. The one of me, my friends, and my parents at my birthday dinner. Everyone was beaming at the camera, and I was leaning over my red velvet cake, about to blow out the big 12 candle.

12.

My twelfth birthday. In August.

A realization made my skin grow warm and prickly. There'd been something else on the website, something besides the list of traits and the "maternal line" thing. I closed my eyes, trying to remember the words.

. . . boys and girls of these ancient families begin showing the above traits at the age of twelve, and become full-fledged vampires shortly thereafter.

My palms went clammy. Of course I still showed up in photographs and in mirrors. Of course I didn't want to suck blood. Of course I didn't turn into a bat. I wasn't a full-fledged vampire.

Yet.

How long was *shortly*? I wondered with growing horror. A few months? Another year? I had no clue, but one thing was certain: At any moment, I could become a full-fledged vampire.

And there was nothing I could do to stop it.

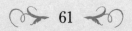

Chapter Six

I had thought it would be difficult going to school with the knowledge that my great-aunt was a vampire.

But that was *nothing* compared to facing school while knowing *I* might be a vampire, too.

As Gabby and I walked to West Side Prep through the brisk morning air, I let my best friend do all the talking. Gabby discussed her braces, Milo from ballet class, and what she should be for Halloween. She'd planned to be a faerie, but now she was considering a werewolf costume, since there was supposed to be a full moon that night.

I knew Gabby was trying to take my mind off things, but all I could think about were dead squirrels and vampire dynasties.

Last night, I'd decided not to tell Gabby about my twelfth-birthday realization. I knew that she would find some logical loophole again, and I didn't have the energy for another therapy session. It felt weird, keeping something so major from my best friend. But I figured I could tell her later on, once *I'd* wrapped my brain around the craziness.

When we got to school, Caitlin and Padma were waiting by our batch of lockers. My stomach sank a little. As much as I liked my friends, I was in no mood for chitchat.

"Hey, girls!" Padma cried, shutting her locker door and tossing her glossy dark braid over one shoulder.

"Feeling better, Emma-Rose?" Caitlin asked earnestly.

"Oh, sure," I replied wryly. "Some might even say I'm fang-tastic."

"What?" Caitlin's fine blond eyebrows came together in confusion.

"Nothing, we all know Em has a twisted sense of humor," Gabby chuckled, elbowing me in the ribs.

"Ow," I pouted, rubbing my side.

"We have time before the first bell," Padma said. "Want to get some hot cocoa from the caf?"

Padma, Gabby, and Caitlin love to drink our cafeteria's hot chocolate in the morning. I prefer a tall glass of cranberry juice.

Which, come to think of it, is red.

Bloodred.

"I can't," I blurted, opening my locker and stuffing my duffel bag inside. "I — um, I need to plan out what I'm doing for my art and drawing class after school."

It was a total lie. From the look she gave me, Gabby knew it was a lie, but I didn't care. I needed to be alone. So I headed for homeroom, where my teacher was shocked that I was not just on time, but early.

First period was social studies, which is usually one of my favorite classes. Today, though, I barely paid attention to Ms. Goldsmith as she talked about the Internet.

"It's a great tool," she said, gesturing with her piece of chalk. "But websites don't always have the most factual data. Sometime before next Monday, I want each of you to pay a visit to your local library. You need to do some good old-fashioned book research on the country of your family's origin."

Thinking about *my* family's origins, I let out a sound that was part laugh, part grunt. Ms. Goldsmith and Padma both looked at me quizzically, so I tried to cover it up by coughing.

Gym class was always torture, but today I was even klutzier than usual. Whenever the volleyball came sailing toward me, I either missed or ducked. And when it was my turn to serve, I couldn't get the ball to go even *near* the net.

"Ugh!" cried Eve Epstein after I'd messed up for the thousandth time. She stamped her metallic pink sneakers, like a toddler throwing a tantrum. "What's the *matter* with you, Emma-Rose? Can't you ever do anything right?"

"Ugh!" echoed Mallory D'Angelo, another one of Ashlee and Eve's obnoxious besties. Mallory wasn't original enough to come up with her own insults.

I glanced at Caitlin, who was also on my team. But my friend could only give me a disappointed frown. Outside of gym, Caitlin is one of the sweetest people alive. In shorts and sneakers, though, the girl becomes an athletic, competitive machine. And I become her embarrassing friend.

I flinched, my throat tightening. *Do* not *cry*, I told myself sternly.

"It's okay!" Coach Lattimore finally called, coming to my rescue. "Better luck next time, Emma-Rose!"

I could tell Caitlin felt bad about gym, because at lunch she bought me a brownie to go with my roast beef sandwich. But I picked listlessly at my food while she, Padma, and Gabby discussed the Halloween dance. As I was chewing, the tip of my tongue touched one of my incisors. It felt very sharp. Sharper than it ever had felt before.

Oh no, I thought. *It's starting.*

Soon, I realized with mounting dread, my ears could shoot out to bat-size. My body could shrink upward and crooked black wings could sprout from my back. I could lunge at one of my friends, determined to pierce their necks and drink . . .

"I — I'll see you guys later," I stammered, stumbling to my feet and dashing out of the cafeteria.

Gabby called after me, but I didn't look back. I knew I was distancing myself from my friends, which made me feel even worse. But eventually, maybe they'd understand that it was for their own safety.

I burst into the girls' room and ran to the mirror, opening my mouth and checking out my incisors. They didn't look longer or pointier than usual. My ears looked normal, and there was nothing growing out of my back. It was also a relief that *I* was still there in the mirror. With shaking fingers, I turned on the faucet and splashed some water on my ashen face.

The door to the girls' room creaked open and in walked Ashlee Lambert, blond hair swinging. When she saw me, she stopped and put one hand on her hip.

"Were you leaving?" she asked me snottily.

Of course Princess Ashlee needed all lowly beings to exit the restroom before she could enter.

"Yes," I replied as coolly as I could, and swept out. I prayed she hadn't seen me examining my fangs. I could just imagine her bringing it up at tomorrow's student council meeting.

As if on cue, Henry Green appeared, strolling lazily down the hall with his books under his arm. When he saw me, a grin spread across his face.

"Hey, Pale Paley!" he called. Instantly, I spun on my heel and marched off in the opposite direction, my heart pounding. *Pale Paley* took on a whole new meaning now that I knew what my paleness was about.

"Hey!" Henry called again as I picked up speed. I thought his voice sounded a little apologetic, but I must have imagined it.

Things didn't get any better as the day progressed. In science, the lesson was on insects, and when my teacher referred to mosquitoes as "thirsty little bloodsuckers," I wanted to crawl under my desk. In English, the discussion was about the Edgar Allan Poe story. My teacher, Ms. Tiller, paced the classroom, talking about fear.

"The scariest thing a writer can create is the feeling of *waiting*," she explained. "You know something horrible is going to happen, but you don't know *when* or *what* exactly it will be."

I began nodding so enthusiastically that I felt like a bobblehead doll. Ms. Tiller raised her eyebrows at me and I stopped nodding. *Someday*, I thought, *there'll be a horror story about* me.

The thought of going home was still terrifying, so I was grateful that I had an after-school activity: my Art & Drawing class at the 92nd Street Y. But my vampire fears followed me there. Our assignment was to draw a self-portrait, and before I knew what I was doing, I had sketched myself with bat wings and bat ears, midmorph. My instructor, Mr. Currin, actually liked my drawing and called it "a fascinating interpretation of the passage from childhood to adulthood." If he only knew the creepy truth.

I wanted to stay at Art & Drawing forever, but I had to go home eventually. My stomach was in knots as I rode the bus across town. As the bus drove through a pale pink, twilit Central Park, I scanned the sky for bats, but I only saw flocks of birds flying south. This gave me the courage I needed to ride the elevator up to my apartment and walk inside, as ready as I'd ever be to face my great-aunt.

But she wasn't there.

"How are you feeling, honey?" Mom asked as she and Dad came out of the kitchen. "You still look a little pale. I bet you and Gabby stayed up too late last night. Should I call Dr. Samuels and make an appointment?"

I shook my head, setting down my duffel bag. I could just imagine my kindly, plump pediatrician starting to take my blood, only to shrink back in horror when he realized I wasn't quite . . . human.

"I feel fine," I lied as Bram ran away from me, whining.

"Did you have a good day at school?" Dad asked.

"It was great," I lied again, glancing around the apartment. "Where's Great-aunt Margo?" I asked.

"She's sleeping," Mom said, coming over to give me a kiss. "She went straight to bed when we got back from the museum. She seemed very tired. Probably jet lag."

Or she's nocturnal, I thought.

"I hope she didn't catch the bug you had yesterday, Emma-Rose," Dad added.

"I think I caught *her*, uh, bug," I mumbled, thinking of bloodsucking mosquitoes.

"What's that?" Mom asked me, straightening my bangs.

"Nothing," I replied distractedly. I wondered if my great-aunt was really asleep or doing something else — some vampire ritual — in the guest room. "I'll be right back," I told my parents, and started down the hall toward my room.

The door to the guest room was ajar, and I dared a glance inside.

Great-aunt Margo was asleep after all, lying flat on her back with her black hair splayed out on the pillow and her pale face motionless. There were no bats in the room, so they must have all been at the museum. I pictured them, somewhere deep inside the building, biding their time in their cages. What would happen when night fell? I felt a tremor of fear for the museum's security guards, whom I'd known forever. Would the bats fly screeching past them into Central Park, or would they use *the guards* for food?

Eek.

I skipped dinner that night.

I also skipped my IM/phone call with Gabby. I still didn't feel ready to tell her everything. So I sent her a text saying I had a lot of homework to do, and she texted back: Okay, but did you talk to Great-aunt Margo?? I sighed and texted back, Not yet.

My plan was to stay up until Great-aunt Margo awoke. Then I'd sneak out of my room to either spy on her or talk to her, depending on how brave I felt. I also wanted to sneak out to the TV and watch the news for any reports on more animal attacks. Plus, there was more research to be done on the Internet. It was going to be a busy night.

But I was exhausted from my crazy day, and I hadn't slept a wink on Gabby's air mattress the night before. I tried to stay awake as I did my homework, but my pencil kept slipping out of my grasp, and my head kept nodding forward.

I'll just stretch out for a little, I thought, flopping onto my bed. And for the first time in a long time, within minutes, I'd fallen fast asleep.

Being a vampire was more tiring than I would have guessed.

Chapter Seven

I tiptoed into the dark, ice-cold room. I hoped no one had followed me. My heart was racing and I wiped my clammy palms on my skirt. I was scared, but I knew I had to go ahead with this. There was no turning back now.

Then, through the blackness, they peered at me: the glowing red eyes. The *hungry* eyes. I had to make myself walk toward them. I had to —

Beep. Beep. Beep!

I reached out and slapped my alarm, burying my face in my pillow.

Wait, I thought, halfway between sleep and waking. *My alarm? It's morning?*

I jolted up, breathless. Sure enough, my room was filled with light. I didn't even think about the

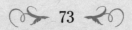

fact that I'd just had my nightmare again. I had to try to catch Great-aunt Margo! Was I too late?

I scrambled out of bed and raced to the guest room. Sure enough, my great-aunt's bed was neatly made, and there was no trace of her.

"She left me a note. She headed out before dawn to get an early start again," Mom explained when I dashed into the kitchen, seeking answers. "Margo's so dedicated."

Before dawn. I shivered.

"But the museum doesn't open until seven for staff, right?" I asked, tugging on my pajama sleeves and staring at Mom intently. "What could she be doing?"

"Well, I imagine she gets breakfast first and maybe walks around a little," Mom said with a shrug as she poured herself a mug of coffee. "She hasn't been to New York in thirteen years, after all. She probably wants to soak up the city."

"Wait — Great-aunt Margo has been here before?" I asked, doing a quick calculation in my head. "Before I was born?"

"Yup," Dad said, glancing up from his cereal bowl. "Mom was pregnant with you at the time.

Margo had come to New York to do some research on bats, but she didn't stay with us back then, since we lived in a much smaller apartment."

Weird. Did Margo's last visit have something to do with the fact that *I* was a vampire? Had she put some sort of spell on Mom while she was pregnant with me?

"Do you have any photos of Great-aunt Margo from then?" I asked, an idea occurring to me. "Or any photos of her *at all*? From when she was my age?"

"Hmm," Mom said, tipping her head to one side. "I actually don't have many photos of Margo. I have some of her as a little girl, but nothing besides that."

Of course not, I thought, gulping. There *wouldn't* be any photos of Great-aunt Margo past the age of twelve. All my suspicions were confirmed.

"You know what, though?" Dad said, putting down his spoon. "I'd bet anything that Margo looked a lot like Emma-Rose when she was young. Did you notice that, Lilly?" he asked Mom. "The resemblance between the two of them is almost . . . spooky."

You have no idea, Dad. You have no idea.

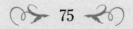

"I did notice," Mom said, smiling at me. "And my mother used to tell me that Margo was always considered their town's great beauty. Hear that, Emma-Rose?"

Me? A beauty? I snorted, glancing down at my tangled hair and pj's.

"It's true," Mom added. "My mother told me that Margo always had young gentleman suitors chasing after her, but she chose not to get married."

Maybe because she couldn't tell any young gentleman the truth about who she was? I wondered. For some reason, I thought of Henry Green, and then pushed his face out of my mind.

"What's with all the interest in Margo, honey?" Dad asked me. "I mean, it's very sweet that you care so much about your great-aunt, but it's a little unlike you."

"Um," I began, feeling trapped. For a second, I thought about opening up and telling my parents the whole spine-chilling truth. But then I remembered how Mom hadn't listened to me on Tuesday morning. And if the three of us got into a discussion about it now, I'd definitely be late for school.

School! I realized, inspired.

"The genealogy project!" I burst out. "I mean . . . yeah, the genealogy project," I said more calmly, because Mom and Dad were looking at me in that worried way again. "For social studies class. I forgot to tell you both about it. We're supposed to research our family history and stuff. So I kind of wanted to interview Great-aunt Margo."

"That's a wonderful idea," Mom said, sipping her coffee. "You may want to wait until after the opening, though. Margo and I will both be swamped until next Friday."

"That reminds me — I have to get my tux dry-cleaned today," Dad said, standing up. "Anything you ladies need dry-cleaned for the gala?"

I bit my lip. In all the insanity of the week, the gala had slipped my mind. I still hadn't decided if I was going to miss it in order to attend the Halloween dance.

The dance. My stomach fell as I remembered that there was a student council meeting that afternoon. Great. That was the *last* thing I needed now. Not that I ever needed — or wanted — student council.

Maybe Gabby was right: Maybe those glowing-eye nightmares were all about Ashlee Lambert and her pink gavel.

I whispered this realization to Gabby as we sat in the back of Classroom 101 at three thirty that afternoon. Ashlee stood at the front of the room, banging away on the desk and calling everyone to order.

"Of course I'm right," Gabby said matter-of-factly, tapping out a text to Caitlin on her cell phone. "Aren't I always?" she added, flashing me a grin as she shut her phone.

I sighed. Gabby had been all chummy with Caitlin at lunch, inviting her over that weekend to play on Carlos's Wii while he was at his karate class. I'd felt a stab of hurt; Gabby had sworn that she and *I* would get to try out the Wii as soon as Carlos stepped away from it. Plus, although Gabby, Caitlin, Padma, and I are all friends, we are also two units of BFFs: Caitlin and Padma, Gabby and Emma-Rose. Period. That's how things work. Padma had seemed miffed, too, but she'd kept quiet, and I'd been in too much of a daze to say anything.

I'd spent the whole day in a daze. Yesterday, people must have figured that I was still recovering from my illness. Today, my teachers all seemed annoyed by my spaciness. I was beginning to worry that vampire or no vampire, I was in danger of flunking the seventh grade.

Henry got up to take attendance, and I felt my cheeks flush. Gabby leaned over to scribble a message in my notebook. I assumed it was about Henry, but instead it read:

Any progress on the great-aunt front?

Nope, I scribbled back. *She sleeps all day and leaves the apartment BEFORE THE SUN COMES UP!*

I was so focused on writing that when Henry called out "Pale Paley?" I flapped my hand in the air without glancing up.

Doesn't mean anyth — Gabby started writing, but then dropped her pencil as a stern voice rang out.

"Emma-Rose! Gabrielle!"

It was Ms. Goldsmith. She stood by our desks, her jaw set.

"Young ladies, I realize we're not in an official class, but no note-writing during student council," she said sternly.

Henry raised his eyebrows, and Ashlee and Eve exchanged triumphant smiles. Anger bubbled up in me. It was totally unfair that Ms. Goldsmith let

Ashlee carry out her little antics but scolded Gabby and me.

"Sorry, Ms. Goldsmith," Gabby said obediently, folding her hands on her desk.

"Sorry," I echoed through gritted teeth. As I looked up at Ms. Goldsmith, my eye landed on the newspaper tucked under her arm. A headline in the lower right-hand corner read: IN CENTRAL PARK, MORE ANIMAL ATTACKS PROMPT QUESTIONS.

My heart somersaulted and my mouth went dry. There *had* been more attacks since Tuesday. I was dying to know what kind of questions had been prompted. Had anyone else in New York City seen the bite marks and realized: Vampire?

I thought about asking Ms. Goldsmith to borrow her paper, or nudging Gabby so that she'd see the headline, but I knew better than to push it.

As Ms. Goldsmith went back to her spot on the windowsill, Ashlee wrote Halloween Dance!! on the chalkboard, her charm bracelet jangling as always. Today, though, the jangling seemed louder than usual. It was giving me a headache.

"Okay!" Ashlee squealed, spinning around. "Today we need to talk about the most fun thing ever — decorations for the dance."

"Ooh!" cried Eve, clapping her hands and making *her* charm bracelet jangle. I massaged my forehead.

"Here's my vision," Ashlee began dramatically, spreading her hands out. "I call it 'Halloween Candy.' We'll have hot-pink balloons and silver streamers. We'll set up cotton candy serving stations, and marshmallow-shaped beanbag chairs. And we could have a red carpet down the middle of the gym, like at celebrity events, only the carpet should be hot-pink, to match the balloons." She paused, then beamed. "Amazing, right?"

"Are you *kidding*?"

The words flew out of my mouth before I could stop them.

Before I'd even realized I'd spoken.

But I *had* spoken.

I'd said, "Are you kidding?" to Princess Ashlee Lambert.

Every single person in the room turned to gawk at me. Me — quiet, meek, Pale Paley, who, up until this moment, hadn't uttered more than three words at a student council meeting. I could feel Gabby's eyes boring into me. Henry, Eve, Roger, Ms. Goldsmith, and all the others stared at me, stunned.

Ashlee crossed her arms over her chest. She lifted her chin, glared at me, and, in the cruelest, coldest voice I'd ever heard, asked, "*What* did you say, Emma-Rose?"

Something came over me then: a rush of warmth and courage I'd never felt before. I was sure it had to do with the events of the past few days. Considering what I'd witnessed in Great-aunt Margo's room on Monday night, it was impossible to feel scared by someone like Ashlee. After all, Ashlee was not a real princess, just a regular seventh grader. But I was the descendant of an ancient, noble line!

Call it vampire-girl-power.

I lifted my chin right back and tossed my dark hair over my shoulder.

"I said," I replied in a clear, even tone. "'Are you kidding?' Because, seriously, Ashlee? Hot-pink and silver for a Halloween dance? That's all wrong."

Gasps and whispers shot through the classroom. Henry's eyes sparkled with mischief, and he leaned against the blackboard, as if enjoying a good show. Eve gaped at me, as if she couldn't believe I had the guts to challenge her leader. Ashlee gaped at me, too, but she quickly collected herself and narrowed her blue eyes.

"Thank you *so* much for sharing your thoughts, Emma-Rose," she said sarcastically. "Do *you* have any brilliant suggestions for the dance's color scheme?" She planted her hands on her hips and curled her glossy upper lip, waiting.

My heart was pounding but in a good, strong way. "Actually, I do," I replied, and in that moment I realized I was full of ideas. I'd been full of them all along, but had never thought to voice my opinions.

"Well, black and orange are the obvious choices, but we could try out some dark reds, too. And," I continued, my confidence growing as I spoke, "we could get permission to put up some cool wall decals, like skulls or cobwebs or ghosts. We should have a smoke machine, and we could fill up a witch's cauldron with candy corn. Or apples to bob for! Oh, and the red carpet idea isn't bad, but we could do even more with that, and have some kids volunteer to be, like, paparazzi and take pictures of all the costumes. It could be a Hollywood Halloween."

I paused for breath. I didn't think I'd ever heard myself say so much. But I didn't feel shy or silly or embarrassed. It had been exciting, letting all my ideas spill out. And it was nice not to be thinking about fangs or dead animals in Central Park.

It was the best I'd felt in days.

The classroom was deathly silent for a moment, and then Gabby turned to me and said in a clear, firm voice, "I think that sounds awesome."

"Thank you," I mouthed, and she gave me a thumbs-up sign.

Of course Gabby would side with me, though; that was a given. When no one else spoke, I began to fidget in my seat and wonder if everyone would shoot down my ideas, especially since Ashlee's face was getting redder by the minute.

But then Henry Green, who'd been standing to the side with his hands in his jeans pockets, stepped forward and cleared his throat.

"Not bad, Pale Paley," he said, with his (annoyingly) cute half smirk. "Not bad at all. Pretty cool, in fact."

I felt myself blush as I shrugged. Ashlee whipped around to glare at Henry, all but screaming the word *Traitor!*

"Yeah," Roger spoke up from his seat. "I really like candy corn."

"And I love wall decals!" exclaimed Zora Robinson. "I bet we can buy temporary ones!"

An excited buzz began to ripple through the room now, with kids turning in their seats to smile at me approvingly. My cheeks grew even hotter.

Ashlee turned away from Henry and zeroed in on Eve, who was nibbling on her hot-pink nails. When Eve opened her mouth to speak, everyone leaned forward to listen.

"I . . . I, um, really like the paparazzi idea?" she said, terror in her eyes.

Ashlee's jaw dropped.

"All right!" someone yelled from across the room, and a smattering of applause broke out. Someone else chanted, "We want Hollywood Halloween!" and someone else said, "Nice going, Emma-Rose!"

I couldn't believe it. I stared at Gabby, who also looked shocked but proud.

"Order!" Ashlee cried, pounding her gavel against the desk. "Order! *I* don't like that idea! Who wants paparazzi at a dance? What's going on here? I'm the president and I get to decide!"

"I'm sorry, Ashlee," Ms. Goldsmith finally spoke, standing up and smoothing out her skirt. "I'm afraid it doesn't work that way. Student council always follows a democratic process, which means the students vote." Before Ashlee could argue, Ms. Goldsmith turned around and faced us. "All in favor of the Halloween Candy idea, please raise your hands," she said.

Ashlee threw her arm into the air with such force she knocked her pink flower ring against the blackboard. Nobody else followed her lead. Hesitantly, Eve raised one hand, but then put it back down on her lap, whispering, "I'm sorry!" to a fuming Ashlee.

"Okay," Ms. Goldsmith said. "All those in favor of Hollywood Halloween?"

Every hand but Ashlee's went into the air. Eve actually raised her arm all the way up, as did Henry and Roger. I felt a burst of pride. I noticed that Ms. Goldsmith was smiling a little, too, and I wondered if, despite scolding me and Gabby before, she was glad to see my idea beat Ashlee's.

"I guess that determines it!" Ms. Goldsmith said, brushing her hands together. "Looks like we're going with Hollywood Halloween."

Ashlee gritted her teeth, smoke practically coming out of her ears.

"And I hereby nominate Emma-Rose the designer-in-chief of the dance!" Gabby called, taking my hand and lifting it up again.

"No — wait, what?" I sputtered, turning to my best friend. "I was just suggesting ideas. . . . I can't actually . . ."

"I second that!" Zora called out, grinning. "You'll do a great job, Emma-Rose."

"Fine," Ashlee spat, throwing down her gavel. "Emma-Rose can be in charge of the design. But that means *you*" — she gave me a withering look — "need to buy all the decorations, *and* set up the gym right before the dance. I'll come to the setup, but only to supervise. I won't want to ruin my nails," she added haughtily.

"I'll help you, obviously," Gabby told me.

"I won't be able to help with the setup," Zora said apologetically. "But I can help you shop for decorations."

"Same here," said Zora's best friend, Janie Woo.

I nodded, feeling a little overwhelmed. What exactly had I gotten myself into?

And then it hit me: If I was in charge of the dance's decorations and design, there was no way I could skip the dance itself.

Which meant that I'd never be able to make the gala.

I felt a pang of disappointment. As Ashlee snippily

adjourned the meeting, Gabby turned to me and saw my frown.

"No gala then, huh?" she said sympathetically. "Or trick-or-treating?"

I shook my head. "I guess Ashlee made the decision for me," I said. "Too bad there's no way for me to dash between the dance and the gala, right?"

"Not unless you can wear a costume to the gala," Gabby sighed.

I watched Ashlee leave the room in a huff, her heels click-clacking. Eve scurried after her, apologizing, and Henry and Roger left as well. As soon as the door shut behind them, all the other kids stood up and began streaming over to my desk.

"Hey, Emma-Rose, it was so cool what you did, standing up to Ashlee!" Zora exclaimed, her eyes bright with admiration.

"Yeah, that pink idea was terrible," groaned Janie.

"We didn't think anyone was going to speak up, though," chimed in a smart guy from my science class named Matt de la Cruz.

"We were *all* rooting for you!" exclaimed another girl, and everyone nodded enthusiastically. Gabby looked as surprised as I felt by all the attention.

"Yes," Ms. Goldsmith said from the front of the classroom, where she was wiping off the chalkboard. She turned around and smiled at me. "I was very impressed by the initiative you showed, Emma-Rose."

"Wow . . . um, thanks," I said. A warm glow spread through me. *Is this what it feels like to be popular?* I wondered.

I didn't feel like myself, but this time it was in a wonderful way.

Maybe becoming a vampire *didn't* totally bite.

Maybe it was even the ticket to becoming a brand-new Emma-Rose!

Chapter Eight

On Friday, I put my New Emma-Rose plan into effect.

I woke up super-early, though not early enough to catch Great-aunt Margo (who had, of course, been asleep again when I'd come home on Thursday afternoon).

I dressed quickly, pairing my dark red jeans with a black tee and a tank top decorated with small red cherries. I added my purple-striped wrist warmers and black boots. Then I texted Gabby to let her know I'd be going ahead to school without her.

I felt a little bad. The two of us hadn't talked or IMed the night before, because Gabby had stayed late at the library doing research for the genealogy project. She'd invited me to join her, but I'd been too hyped up from student council and had instead gone shopping for dance decorations with Zora. There was now a bag in the corner of my room overflowing with sparkly skull decals and orange and black crepe streamers.

I stopped by the kitchen, surprising Mom. Dad was still asleep. As I poured myself a glass of cranberry juice, I broke the news that I wouldn't be able to make the gala on Friday. Mom was disappointed, but told me she was proud of me for getting involved in the school dance.

The first people I saw at school were Eve, Mallory, Roger, and Henry. They were standing in front of their lockers, and I heard Eve telling the guys that Ashlee was out sick. I wondered if the little princess had needed a day to recover from the shock of student council.

As I headed for my locker, Henry called out, "Morning, Pale Paley!"

I whipped around and shot him the kind of glare I imagined a powerful girl vampire would shoot a helpless squirrel. I didn't blush. I didn't squirm.

"You know what?" I said firmly. "That's getting really old."

Henry blinked, then pushed a hand through his dark hair. "Um," he said nervously.

Eve, Mallory, and Roger exchanged glances. They, too, weren't used to me speaking up — or speaking much at all. I wouldn't let any of them off the hook, but stood my ground, hands on my hips.

Finally, Mallory offered me a cautious smile and said, "Hey, Emma-Rose. I like your outfit."

"Thanks," I replied. Before I turned to my locker, I saw Eve elbowing Mallory.

"What?" Mallory whispered. "It's cute."

I smiled to myself.

Once gym class rolled around, I knew Mallory's semisweetness wouldn't last. She and I were on the same team again, along with Eve and Caitlin. Last time, we had lost — because of me. Today, Eve and Caitlin, though far from being friends, seemed to agree that they would do whatever it took to win. When the other team served the ball, they both lunged. Caitlin bumped the ball toward Eve, who spiked it over the net.

"Go, Eve!" Mallory screamed. "Go, Caitlin," she added halfheartedly.

Coach Lattimore blew her whistle. "ROTATE!" she called. My stomach twisted up in knots. It was my turn to serve.

"Now, remember what I told you, Emma-Rose," Coach Lattimore said, coming over to stand next to me. She placed the ball — my enemy — in my hand. "Use force. Use *all* your strength. And get that ball *over* the net."

"Come on, Coach L, can't she just skip serving?" Eve moaned.

"Shh, it'll be funny at least," I heard Mallory hiss.

I saw Caitlin studying her sneakers, as if she couldn't bear to see me fail again.

And just like that, the rush of power I had felt in student council yesterday came surging back. What was I so worried about? I was a *vampire*. What was volleyball compared to hunting creatures in the dead of the night?

I could do this. I could *so* do this.

My blood was roaring in my ears. I swung my arm back, and my fist connected with the ball, sending it forward with such speed that I gasped. The ball cleared the net and zoomed over the heads of the other team. One girl dove for it, but she missed, and the ball hit the floor.

There was a stunned silence.

The whistle fell out of Coach Lattimore's mouth.

"Yay, Emma-Rose!" Caitlin shrieked, running over to give me a hug. I hugged Caitlin back, grinning so wide my face hurt.

"Go, Emma-Rose!" a few other teammates joined in, clapping. I had never imagined I would hear that sound, and I soaked in the joy of victory.

Even better was the sight of Eve and Mallory, standing still, their faces pale. They exchanged a bewildered glance, then stared back at me.

I couldn't resist. "Thanks for all the support, guys!" I told them. Caitlin cracked up, and even Coach Lattimore chuckled.

After class, I returned to the locker room, sweaty and smiling. When I glanced into the mirror above the sinks, I was almost disappointed to see that I didn't have fully grown fangs yet.

So this is what it's like to be something more than human, I thought, standing tall. For the first time since I'd realized what I was, I could feel the ancient magic of my ancestors running through my veins.

* * *

At the end of the day, I pushed open the school doors, my arms feeling strong and my hair swishing back and forth like black silk. The cloudy sky only made me smile wider. I walked with confidence down the steps, still energized. I could easily play another volleyball game.

"Em! Wait up!"

I turned around to see Gabby jogging toward me, her curls and backpack bouncing.

I waved, happy to see her. We hadn't had a chance to catch up during lunch, because Zora, Matt, and Janie had sat at our table to update me on the dance decorations. Matt had gotten some sixth graders to volunteer to be paparazzi, and Zora and Janie had found a cauldron at a Halloween store downtown. I'd expected Gabby to join in the conversation, but she'd seemed more interested in talking to Caitlin and Padma.

"Look what I got you," Gabby said when she reached my side, pulling a small plastic bag out of her backpack. "I meant to give this to you earlier today."

"A gift?" I laughed, accepting the bag from Gabby. "What's the occasion?"

"I just thought you could use a pick-me-up." Gabby grinned.

"Oh. I've actually been —" The words stuck in my throat when I shook the contents of the bag into my hand.

Gabby had gotten me a pair of plastic fangs.

"Funny, right?" Gabby giggled, her brown eyes sparkling.

I frowned at my best friend. In that moment, she seemed almost like a stranger. *Funny?* Nothing about the situation was a joke to me.

"Yeah, hilarious," I answered wryly, shoving the fangs into my book bag. Without meeting Gabby's gaze, I turned and walked away from the school. Red and gold leaves crunched beneath my feet.

Gabby fell into step beside me, and was quiet for a moment, as if unsure what to say next. "You're still coming over, right?" she finally asked.

"Sure," I replied, even though I'd sort of forgotten that it was Friday and I always went to Gabby's place on Friday afternoons. "Did you invite Caitlin, too?" I added, then regretted my words when I saw the wounded look on Gabby's face.

"No." Gabby's voice sounded a little curt. "Why would I?"

"Well, isn't she coming over to play on Carlos's Wii tomorrow?" I said, hearing the sharpness in my voice.

Gabby nodded sheepishly as we headed west along 83rd Street. "She is. Padma can't make it because she has piano lessons. But you should come, too, Em!" she added hurriedly. "I'm sorry I didn't invite you before — you've seemed really distracted lately. Like you'd almost rather be alone."

"Yeah, I know," I said, fighting a wave of guilt as we sidestepped a cluster of pigeons.

"Is it because of that whole 'vampire' thing?" Gabby asked with a half smile, making air quotes with her fingers.

I stopped walking. Maybe it had to do with her fangs-are-funny! gift, or her light tone, but suddenly I was really annoyed.

"Would you keep it down?" I whispered, glancing over my shoulder. The Museum of Natural History was close by. Margo herself could appear at any moment, fangs out and wings spread. The thought made my whole body turn rigid with terror.

"I knew it," Gabby sighed, putting her hands on her hips. "I knew you were still obsessing. I bet you haven't talked to Great-aunt Margo yet. Probably because you know she'll give you a logical explanation, and you don't *want* that!"

My patience snapped. "No," I hissed. "I haven't talked to her because she's totally nocturnal, okay? Oh, and remember how you tried to convince me that I don't have any of those *symptoms*? Well, you were wrong."

Keeping my voice as low as possible, I explained to Gabby about my twelfth birthday realization. I waited for my best friend's eyes to widen with fear. For her to apologize for doubting me.

Instead, she rolled her eyes.

"That doesn't prove anything," she scoffed. "Just because it happened to say that on *one* website . . ." She shook her head as we stopped on the corner to wait for the light. "I wish you'd told me that earlier. I could have saved you a lot of stress."

Thunder rumbled overhead. I stared hard at Gabby, at her superior expression and her arms folded smugly over her chest. *Has she ever really understood me?* I wondered.

"*This* is why I didn't tell you," I retorted. "Because I knew you'd act like this. I knew you wouldn't really believe me."

I realized that I'd known all along that Gabby

would dismiss whatever I said. But wasn't a best friend supposed to stand by you no matter what?

"I'm only trying to help," Gabby protested, raising her voice over the honking of car horns. "I mean, come on, Em. You've been a mess all week!"

I felt a pinprick of hurt. *You are a descendant of an ancient dynasty*, I reminded myself. I heard another threatening roar of thunder.

"I may have been acting a little weird," I retorted. "But I'm better now. Actually, I'm doing great, in case you didn't notice."

"Oh, I've noticed," Gabby snapped as we crossed the street. Her cheeks were pink, a sure sign that something was bothering her. "I've noticed how all you care about now is being the most popular girl in student council, and being friends with eighth graders, and —"

"What?" I stopped in the middle of the street, and Gabby had to tug on my arm to pull me forward. My skin was flushed with anger as we reached the curb. I'd been feeling so good about myself all day, and now Gabby was ruining everything. "I thought — I thought you were *happy* for me. You nominated me designer-in-chief!"

My stomach tightened. Suddenly, it seemed like our conversation was spinning out of control. Spinning in a direction that was somehow even scarier than vampires.

"Well, I never expected it to go to your head like this!" Gabby shot back.

As if shocked by her words, the sky opened up and the first raindrops began to fall on us. I'd been in such a rush that morning I'd forgotten to bring an umbrella.

"I can't believe it," I muttered. "You're totally jealous! That's what this is about."

Gabby rolled her eyes again.

"You're jealous," I repeated. "Because *I'm* finally standing up to people and speaking my mind; and *you* haven't even worked up the nerve to talk to Milo in ballet class!" I was practically shouting now.

A hurt look crossed Gabby's face, and I bit my bottom lip. I hadn't meant to bring up boys, or to sound so mean.

"Whatever," Gabby spat. "*You'll* never admit that you like Henry Green. But then again, if he found out you thought you were a *you-know-what*, he'd never like *you*!"

I gasped. How had this happened so quickly? Gabby and I had gone from being BFF to saying awful things to each other. I wanted to reverse everything, to reach out and hug her and apologize. But it felt like it was too late.

The rain was coming down harder now. All around us people were opening their umbrellas, but Gabby and I stood still, getting drenched.

"I don't care," I said firmly, meaning it. "I don't care what you think, Gabby."

Gabby set her jaw. "I feel the same way, Emma-Rose."

Emma-Rose. The name was a punch in the gut. Gabby never called me that. I was always "Em" to her. I fought down the lump in my throat.

"Fine," I snapped, my voice catching. "I guess I won't come over, then."

"Fine!" Gabby snapped back, her own eyes looking bright with tears — though it could have been the rain.

"Fine," I repeated, just for good measure.

Then I whipped around so fast that I almost knocked into someone's umbrella. I started back across the street, toward home. I was shaking. In all our seven years of friendship, Gabby and I had never fought this way.

"Oh, and you can forget about me helping you set up before the dance!" Gabby shouted after me.

"I don't need you, anyway!" I shouted back. Then I broke into a run, my feet slamming into the pavement as the rain pounded down on me. I ran with all the vampire strength I could summon. I was winded and soaked when I reached my building.

And then I realized something that made the lump in my throat grow bigger: Gabby was the only one who'd known — and, up until a few minutes ago, cared — about my secret. Caitlin and Padma would probably side with Gabby if asked to choose. My new student council friends would freak if I told them what I really was. My parents were no help. And Great-aunt Margo was too busy turning into a bat, attacking helpless animals, or hiding from the sun to talk to me.

I took a deep breath and walked into my building.

I was on my own.

Chapter Nine

"Hello, dah-link!"

Stepping inside my apartment, I nearly had a heart attack at the sight of Great-aunt Margo. She was striding toward me, carrying one of her luxurious leather suitcases in one hand and a large black umbrella in the other.

I froze, rainwater dripping off me and onto the foyer rug. All thoughts of Gabby and the fight fled my mind.

It was the first time I'd seen my great-aunt since that stormy Monday night. My eyes swept over her, searching for signs of the fearsome bat. Her face was as pale as ever, except for her bright red mouth and her navy blue eyes. Her dark hair was piled on top of her head, and she wore a chic black trench coat and high-heeled black boots.

No wings. No fangs. For now.

"Vy do you look so frightened, my dear?" Great-aunt Margo laughed, flashing her very white teeth. "It is only me!"

She really doesn't know, I thought, amazed. *She doesn't know that I know . . .*

"I . . . I . . . you . . ." I cleared my throat. "Are you going back to Romania?" was all I could manage, pointing to her suitcase.

I felt a mix of worry and relief. On the one hand, she was leaving, right when I could ask her everything! At the same time, I sort of wanted her to disappear, taking along with her all the problems she had brought me.

"Not yet, dah-link," Great-aunt Margo replied, walking right up to me. I cowered but she didn't seem to notice. She kissed my cheek, and her lips felt like ice. "I am just going to a spa for a few days," she explained. "In Pennsylvania."

I'd never thought of it before, but *Pennsylvania* sounds a lot like *Transylvania*.

I heard a whimpering sound, and noticed that

Bram was all the way down the hall near my parents' bedroom, clearly waiting for Great-aunt Margo to leave.

"I must get some rest and beautifying before the gala on Friday," Great-aunt Margo continued, heading for the door. "Your mother and father know I vill be gone for a vile. They are off having dinner vit friends tonight."

I spun around. "Wait!" I cried after her, feeling desperate.

Great-aunt Margo turned back to me, raising her brows. "Yes, dah-link?"

I opened my mouth. A million questions flooded my brain.

What have you and your bats been up to every night?

Are you only going outside now because it's gray and raining?

Are you good at volleyball?

When will I become a full-fledged vampire?

But somehow the words never made it off my tongue. All I could get out was:

"When will you . . . will I . . . will you have a good time?"

So much for being brave and speaking my mind.

"Oh, I vill, dah-link, thank you," Great-aunt Margo purred as she opened the door. "You make sure you get enough rest, too. Next Friday vill be a big night for you!"

Before I could tell my great-aunt that I wouldn't be going to the gala, she had swept out of the apartment. Only a cloud of flowery perfume lingered in her wake. Bram let out a bark that sounded sort of like "Good riddance!" And I stood there in my wet clothes, still brimming with unanswered questions.

"I have a question," I whispered to the librarian.

It was the next afternoon, and I was at my local library. I'd woken up depressed, thinking about all the things I should have asked Great-aunt Margo, and imagining how much fun Gabby and Caitlin were having without me. When Mom found me moping, she told me to do something "productive," and I remembered that we were supposed to visit the library for Ms. Goldsmith's class. It was not the coolest way to spend a Saturday, but I guess that's what happens when you're a vampire who's just lost your best friend.

The librarian, a skinny young man with black-framed glasses, glanced up from his computer screen.

"Yes?" he asked me in a normal voice.

I was surprised. I'd thought librarians were supposed to whisper. "I'm looking for books on Transyl — on Romania," I corrected myself, making sure to whisper.

"Got it, Romania," the librarian said briskly. His words sounded like a shout in the silent room. I cringed, and he pointed me toward a set of bookshelves nearby.

"Thank you," I mouthed, turning to go.

Then I paused. Out of all the cruel things Gabby had said to me yesterday, one in particular was sticking in my head, refusing to go away:

Just because it happened to say that on one website . . .

I hated to admit it, but my ex-BFF had a point. I'd been basing all my theories on that one site about Transylvanian vampires. Hadn't Ms. Goldsmith said that the Internet wasn't always the most reliable source? Maybe thick, old, dusty books would hold more answers. That was always the way it worked in *Harry Potter*, anyway.

I turned back to the librarian, leaned forward, and whispered extra-quietly, "Where would I find books on vamp — vamp —" I couldn't get the word out.

"Vampires?" the librarian all but yelled. "Right over there!" He pointed to another section of the room, in the far, far back.

I held my breath and turned to look at the people sitting at the tables. I was sure they'd all be glaring at me or waving knobs of garlic in the air. Miraculously, everyone was still bent over their laptops and books. I let out a shaky sigh of relief.

I swung by the Romania shelves, but I couldn't concentrate on any of the books there when I knew there was vampire knowledge waiting across the room. So I hurried past Mr. Loud Librarian and into the vampire section.

Here, the library seemed dimmer. My heart began to beat faster. I came to a row of shelves marked FOLKLORE AND LEGENDS. I thought I heard footsteps on the other side of the shelf, but I hoped I was imagining it. I wanted to be alone in this little nook.

I scanned the different titles. There were books on ghouls, zombies, unicorns, and mermaids. Finally,

I located three vampire books. One was called *In the Blood: Vampire Facts and Fables*. Another was called *Fangs for the Memories: Vampires in Literature and Pop Culture*. The third was called simply *The Vampyre* and was so old that the dark red spine was cracked, and the letters of the title were peeling off.

I decided to take all three books. But once they were in my arms, they seemed to weigh a ton. I staggered a little. I was trying to balance the books and walk at the same time when a teasing, familiar voice spoke up from behind me.

"Need a hand there, Pale Paley?"

The books all fell with a loud crash. The people at the tables turned and shot me annoyed looks. Mr. Loud Librarian had the nerve to hold his finger to his mouth and say, "Shhh!"

Slowly, Henry Green walked around so that he was facing me. His eyes sparkled.

"I guess the answer is yes," he said.

My cheeks got so warm I was worried my face would burst into flames.

Henry Green?

He was the absolute last person I'd ever have expected to bump into at the library. I wished I could sneak off and text Gabby about this surprise run-in, but then I remembered that we weren't speaking.

"No, I don't need a hand," I snapped in a mortified whisper. But Henry was already kneeling down and scooping up the fallen books.

"Okay, what's on the reading list?" he asked, looking at each title. "*In the Blood*? *The Vampyre*?"

Panic washed over me. "Stop it!" I hissed, trying to snatch the books back, but he held them out of my reach. I didn't want to make a scene, so I gave up. Henry got to his feet, smiling triumphantly. I gritted my teeth.

"Why are you even here?" I demanded, trying to keep my voice to a whisper. "Shouldn't you be at soccer practice or something?"

"Not today," Henry replied matter-of-factly, adjusting his messenger bag across his chest and tucking my vampire books under his arm. "I was doing research for Ms. Goldsmith's class." I noticed that two library books were sticking out from the top of his unzipped bag; one looked to be on France, the other on Russia. "But I got bored and came to see if they had anything interesting in this section."

"*You* . . . you're interested in this stuff?" I asked, gesturing to the FOLKLORE AND LEGENDS sign. I took in

Henry's West Side Prep soccer hooded sweatshirt, khakis, and Adidas sneakers. I'd always assumed he was only into sports and video games and being Mr. Popularity.

Then again, I'd never really gotten to know him.

"Yeah, totally." Henry grinned. I realized that, for once, he wasn't speaking to me in a teasing or mocking way. "You should see my collection of old-school horror movies at home — I mean, um —" Quickly, Henry ducked his head and shuffled his Adidas.

I squinted at him, confused. Was he . . . *blushing*? No. It couldn't be. And he hadn't just sort of invited me over to his house, had he? No. It couldn't be.

"I also have a tarantula," he announced, glancing up again. Instantly, he looked embarrassed at having told me this random fact. "But you probably hate tarantulas, huh?"

"Nope," I replied, shrugging. "They're kind of cool."

As long as I don't have any relatives who are secretly tarantulas, I thought.

"Really?" Henry asked. "Don't girls think all bugs are gross? Ashlee does."

The way he said Ashlee's name — in a kind of fed-up tone — made me wonder if he wasn't her biggest fan. Another surprise. I'd always assumed Henry liked her. The crush type of *like*.

"Well, I'm pretty different from Ashlee, in case you haven't noticed," I said. I couldn't keep myself from smiling.

Meanwhile I was thinking: *Am I really standing here, having a conversation with Henry Green?* It definitely wasn't the strangest thing to have happened to me this week, but it was up there.

"I've noticed," Henry laughed. "I mean, you had all those smart ideas for the Halloween dance."

"Oh. Um, thanks." My heart did a funny flip-flop. I looked down at my boots, my hair falling over my face. Had he just complimented me? Weird.

"Is that what these are for?" Henry asked, holding up my vampire books. "Research for Halloween?"

I shifted from one foot to the other. "You could say that," I replied. *Though I can use them for my genealogy project, too.*

"Were you gonna sit down?" Henry asked, and he jutted his chin toward a small table nestled in the corner behind us.

"Uh, that was the plan," I replied. And surprise number three about Henry Green was that he carried my books over to the table and set them down for me.

I waited for him to tease me about something, but he was actually being polite and, well, nice. Almost like a friend. I wondered if it was because I'd barked at him yesterday for calling me Pale Paley. Or maybe getting away from school and his popular crew made him act a little differently. In a good way.

I expected Henry to say bye and take off, maybe to meet Roger or someone for a movie. Instead, he stood still, examining the titles of my books again.

"So, what's with the vampire fascination?" he asked, smiling.

Oh, boy.

I gulped, tucking my hair behind my ears. "I guess it's a subject that, um, hits close to home," I managed to reply, hoping Henry couldn't hear the thudding of my heart.

Henry nodded, his green eyes bright. "Okay, speaking of vampires?" he began. He glanced over his shoulder, then took a step closer to me. I felt myself blush again. "I haven't told this to anyone, but do you wanna hear something crazy?" he whispered.

"Sure?" I squeaked out. What could Henry possibly tell me that was crazier than my own story?

"I have this theory," Henry whispered. "Have you been hearing about the dead squirrels and birds they've been finding in Central Park every night?" I nodded, feeling like I might pass out. "Well," Henry continued, looking thoughtful. "I know it's insane, but to me, it sounds almost like the animals are being attacked by vampires. I mean, the two-pronged bites on the neck? That's a classic vampire mark. Don't you think?"

The bookshelves around me began to spin. My hands and feet turned cold.

"People have been saying it's a hawk," Henry went on, his eyes wide. "But come *on*. It's not a hawk. I think . . . I *bet* . . ." He lowered his voice even more. "There are vampires in Manhattan."

All the blood drained from my face. Without warning, my knees buckled and I sank into the chair at the table.

Henry frowned at me. "Whoa, are you okay? I'm sorry if I freaked you out." He shook his head. "This is why I haven't told anyone! I guess I thought you'd maybe understand since you seem into vampires and —"

"I understand," I interrupted.

Henry raised his eyebrows. "You do?"

I looked up at Henry, taking note of the sincerity in his eyes. In an afternoon full of surprises, the biggest one was this: that, suddenly, Henry Green, of all people, seemed like someone I could confide in.

The bravery I'd felt in school yesterday swept over me. Maybe I didn't have to be totally "on my own" without Gabby. Maybe I could share my secret with the most unlikely person in the world.

I took a deep breath. I knew I might be making a huge mistake. I knew I was running the risk that Henry would tell Ashlee and Eve and Roger and all of West Side Prep about me. But I was willing to take that risk, because I sensed that Henry would believe what I was about to say.

"I understand," I repeated. "Because I am one."

Chapter Ten

Henry didn't say anything at first. He just took off his messenger bag and sat down in the chair across from me. Then he leaned forward, put his elbows on the table, and gave me a serious look.

"Tell me everything," he whispered.

I didn't trust my voice to work, so I reached into my backpack and pulled out my social studies notebook and a pen. As Henry waited, I wrote down all the events of my wild week. I left out the part about fighting with Gabby, and my volleyball victory, sticking mainly to the Great-aunt Margo details. Somehow, putting everything into writing made me feel lighter and freer. It felt almost as good as drawing.

When I was done, I flexed my cramped fingers and pushed the paper across the table to Henry.

He read it carefully, his green eyes darting over my messy handwriting, and I held my breath.

A small part of me was terrified that he, like Gabby, would scoff at my all-too-true tale of bats and dynasties and Transylvania. There was also the possibility that he would laugh, summon Ashlee out of a hiding place, and, in his usual teasing voice, tell me it had all been a giant prank. *Or* his face would turn white, and he would jump up and stumble away, disgusted by me.

But as soon as he finished reading, he passed the paper back to me. Then he looked me in the eye and asked, "So how do we find out when you become full-fledged?"

It might have been the fact that he said *we* that made me want to get up and throw my arms around him. Fortunately, I resisted.

"Thank you," I said instead, hoping Henry could see the gratitude written on my face. I took the piece of paper from him and crumpled it up, shoving it deep inside my backpack. "For not running away or something," I added.

"Are you kidding?" Henry shook his head, his eyes dancing with excitement. "I always *knew* that things like this existed in real life. But I never really talk about it with my friends. I once tried to ask Roger if he believed in ghosts, and he told me I was being a dork." He rolled his eyes.

"Well, you are a dork, but that's beside the point," I replied. It was fun to tease Henry back for once.

Henry grinned. "Hey, now. Just because you're a fledgling vampire doesn't mean you can get all evil."

My ears pricked up. "Fledgling?" I whispered. "Is that what I am?"

"I think so," Henry said, reaching for the book called *In the Blood*. "I read a book like this one last year, and it said that vampires who haven't really matured yet are known as fledglings." He furrowed his brow, opening the book and skimming the first page. "I can't remember, but I'm pretty sure there's some kind of moment, or ritual, when the fledglings reach maturity and can morph into bats and stuff."

"Really?" I whispered, my stomach tightening. "A ritual?" I grabbed the *Fangs for the Memories* book. "Maybe one of these books will tell us more."

"Let's see," Henry said, looking determined.

Hidden away in the dark, dusty corner of the library, Henry and I got down to business. Henry tackled *In the Blood* while I tore through *Fangs for the Memories*, each of us passing the books back and forth when we found anything that caught our attention.

Fangs for the Memories didn't offer much more than lists of different vampire movies and books through the ages. Henry told me he owned most of the movies, and that we could watch them for research if we needed to.

In the Blood didn't say much more about vampire traits than the website had. I learned, however, that hungry vampire bats often had red eyes, and that the Romanian word for vampire was *nosferatu*, which somehow sounded even scarier.

But it was in the crumbling, yellowing pages of *The Vampyre* that we hit pay dirt. There was a chapter in the book called "The Dynasties of Transylvania." Henry moved his chair around the table next to me so we could read it together.

The chapter talked about the mysterious beauty of the Carpathian Mountains and the ancient vampire bloodlines of the region. I got so wrapped up that I forgot to feel nervous that Henry and I were sitting side by side.

Not that I cared.

Right?

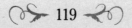

When we came to the second page of the chapter, Henry gasped, and pointed to a paragraph that made my skin freeze:

Every vampyre is familiar with the annual, all-important nocturne ritual. Fledglings receive a special summoning to this ancient rite, and are required to attend. It is there, among legions of full-fledged vampyres, that fledglings make their first transformation into great winged bats.

"We found it!" Henry exclaimed, forgetting to whisper. "That's the ritual I was thinking of!"

"The Nocturne Ritual," I murmured, the name making me shiver. Our corner of the library suddenly seemed a little cooler and a little darker than it had before.

Across the room, Mr. Loud Librarian cleared his throat and glared in our direction. Henry and I glanced over at him for a second, then shrugged at each other and delved back into the book:

Presided over by the empress of vampyres, the nocturne ritual takes place on the night of

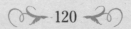

the autumn's second full moon. The event is
shrouded in careful secrecy: It is held in a dif-
ferent, distant land each year, and thirteen
years must pass before the ritual can take place
in the same land again. The ritual is held
indoors, often in the midst of a great ball or
celebration. If there are human imposters pres-
ent, they will instantly be identified, as they
will not be able to shape-shift into bats.

"Sounds intense," Henry said.

I leaned back in my chair, trying to work out all the details in my mind.

"A distant land?" I said, overwhelmed. "How am I supposed to even get to the ritual? I'm not allowed to take an airplane by myself."

"Well, it's a land distant from *Transylvania*," Henry pointed out, running his finger over the text. "Which could be anywhere. It *could* even be right here in New York City."

A memory was nagging at me. There was something someone had said to me recently, about New York City, and thirteen years. What *was* it? I closed my eyes and tried hard to recall the conversation.

"What are you thinking?" Henry asked me.

"I'm thinking that the two of you are being very disruptive."

Mr. Loud Librarian's voice made both of us jump. My eyes flew open and I saw him standing by our table with a disapproving look on his face.

"You have not been speaking at a library-appropriate volume," he said, wagging a finger at us. "I'm afraid I'm going to have to ask you to take your little study group elsewhere."

Seriously? Henry and I exchanged a glance. The man with the loudest voice on the planet was telling *us* we were being too noisy? It would have been funny if it weren't totally ruining our research.

"Sorry about that," Henry said, hiding his smile as we stood and gathered our books. Griping about Mr. L. L., we took the elevator down to the main lobby, where Henry checked out his genealogy books, and I checked out *The Vampyre*. Then we exited the library and stepped into the blinding sunshine.

As Henry and I crossed the street, I reached into my book bag for my sunglasses. But before I could put them on, I saw something that made me stop dead in my tracks.

On the corner was a newsstand with an orange and black ad on its side. The ad read:

BATS AND POSSUMS AND OWLS, OH MY!

COME DISCOVER:

CREATURES OF THE NIGHT

OPENING SATURDAY, NOVEMBER 1

THE AMERICAN MUSEUM OF NATURAL HISTORY

79TH STREET AND CENTRAL PARK WEST

My pulse began to pound.

The exhibit. Great-aunt Margo. Her bats. New York City.

That was what I'd been trying to recall: a conversation about Great-aunt Margo! On Thursday morning, Mom had told me that Margo had been in New York City thirteen years ago.

Thirteen years.

And hadn't that elderly lady said something on the news? Something about similar animal attacks in Central Park happening thirteen years ago?

I started to tremble. That was *it*. It had to be.

"Hey, what's wrong?" Henry asked, clearly seeing my stunned expression.

I turned to face him. "I think . . . I think I just figured something out."

Without a word, Henry and I sat down on the closest bench, and I took *The Vampyre* out of my book bag. Quickly, I flipped to the page we'd been on before, and read out loud:

"'Thirteen years must pass before the ritual can take place in the same land again. The ritual is held indoors, often in the midst of a great ball or celebration.'"

I glanced up at Henry, excitement and fear building in me. "Henry, my great-aunt was last in New York City thirteen years ago, and I'm pretty sure there were other vampires with her at the time. I don't know what kind of celebration or ball was going on then, but she *is* attending a big celebration now! The opening gala for the Creatures of the Night exhibit is this Halloween, at the Museum of Natural History!"

Henry's eyes were growing wider by the second. "Halloween?" he whispered. "There's a blood moon this Halloween!"

"What's a blood moon?" I asked, hugging my arms to keep from trembling.

"That's what people sometimes call October's or

November's full moon, because of its reddish color," Henry explained. "But listen . . . since there was already a full moon in September, October thirty-first will be *autumn's second full moon*!"

Henry and I stared at each other in shocked silence.

It made sense. All of it. The gala would provide the perfect distraction, and the museum was huge, with plenty of places to hide. My mind raced as I pictured all the different rooms and halls. There were the dinosaurs, the animal dioramas, the giant blue whale, and the planetarium. *Where would the ritual take place?* I wondered.

"But wait," Henry said, breaking into my thoughts. "Shouldn't you have received your 'summoning' or whatever by now?"

I imagined receiving a fancy invitation in the mail, with the words *You Are Cordially Invited to the Nocturne Ritual* written out in blood. I shuddered.

"Has your great-aunt mentioned the gala to you specifically?" Henry asked.

"She and I haven't even talked all that much," I sighed. "Just when she first arrived, and then yesterday afternoon when she . . ." I trailed off.

What had Great-aunt Margo said to me as she'd left for her spa?

Next Friday vill be a big night for you!

My heart skipped a beat. I'd thought she was just referring to the gala, but she'd meant something else entirely.

I repeated the words to Henry, and he nodded. "That was totally your summoning," he confirmed. "So now we know for sure."

I nodded dazedly. Then I looked down at my arms — arms that would soon be glossy black wings. I touched my cheek — soon, a bat face. I felt my incisor with the tip of my tongue, imagining the fangs that would shoot out. All of it was actually going to happen. I was going to become a full-fledged vampire.

Talk about a big night.

"Crazy, huh?" Henry murmured. I could tell he thought it was cool that I'd be embarking on this adventure. Meanwhile, I wasn't sure how I felt about any of it.

"Are you gonna be okay going to the museum alone?" Henry was asking me. "Maybe some friends should come with you and stand guard or something?"

"Maybe," I said.

Wait.

My heart dropped like a stone.

In all the excitement of the afternoon, I had completely forgotten.

"Except there's one big catch." I sighed, slumping back against the bench.

"What?" Henry looked worried.

"The Halloween dance!" I cried. "It's at the exact same time. And you heard Ashlee. Now that I'm doing the decorations, I *have* to be there."

"But you can't miss the Nocturne Ritual either," Henry pointed out, taking *The Vampyre* from me. "It says fledglings are 'required' to attend."

"I know," I groaned, burying my face in my hands. My old problem was back to haunt me — big-time.

"Unless . . ." Henry began.

I looked up at him, feeling a prickle of hope.

"Unless you put up all the decorations superfast, and then run over to the museum," Henry said. "It's only two blocks from school."

I brushed my bangs off my forehead, doubtful. How could I transform the whole gym into Hollywood Halloween and make it to my vampire initiation in time, especially now that Gabby had bailed on me?

"I'll help you," Henry offered.

I whipped my head around to look at him in surprise. "You will?"

"I mean, I'm not really good at putting up decorations or whatever," Henry said with a half smile. "But I can try. And I can distract Ashlee with a few vice presidential questions when you need to leave."

I frowned at Henry. I was grateful, but also confused.

"I don't get it," I said flatly. It must have been the new, powerful Emma-Rose that was letting me talk so plainly. "Why — why are you being . . . nice to me? All you do at school is make fun of me and call me Pale Paley."

Henry's face flushed, and he ran a hand through his hair, looking unsettled. "I, um, I want to know how this whole vampire thing turns out," he stammered, not really answering my question. He glanced at his watch. "Anyway, I'm supposed to meet Roger now to play some soccer in the park," he said.

I looked at my watch, too. "Oh, right," I gasped. "I have to meet my dad." He would be waiting in front of the library by now to walk me home.

We stood up, and Henry handed me back *The*

Vampyre. "Um, so, good luck," he added. "I guess we can talk more about this at school if we need to."

"I guess," I said, still feeling bewildered about everything. I waved to Henry, turned, and started to walk away.

"Hey, Emma-Rose?" he called after me. I glanced at him over my shoulder. "I won't tell anyone about this," he said, his green eyes solemn. "I promise."

Emma-Rose?

I blinked.

He called me Emma-Rose?

"Thanks," I choked out, then turned away again, my mind reeling. It was the first time Henry Green had ever spoken my real name.

But I couldn't focus on Henry now. There were more urgent matters at hand.

Like the fact that, in less than a week, my life would be changed forever.

Chapter Eleven

A blur. That was the best way to describe the days leading up to Halloween.

On Sunday, every time I tried to read *The Vampyre*, I became so nervous about the Nocturne Ritual that I had to set the book aside. Next, I wrote a half-apologetic, half-angry e-mail to Gabby, but couldn't work up the courage to send it. Finally, I drew some sketches that may or may not have included Henry Green's face.

Monday morning, I was awakened by my cell phone's beep. It was a text message from Gabby, but to my disappointment, she wasn't writing to say she was sorry. She had sent the coldest message in the history of texting:

Won't b picking u up.

Fine by me! I texted back, pressing the keys so hard I almost broke my phone.

Fine, Gabby responded, just to get in the last word, I'm sure.

I fumed as I wolfed down my sausages. When Mom and Dad asked me what was wrong, I told them Gabby and I had had a "misunderstanding" and left it at that. I didn't want to burden my parents with my Gabby issues, considering they'd soon have a full-fledged vampire living under their roof.

Will I be a danger to them? I wondered as I walked to school with Dad, keeping a safe distance from him on the street. I couldn't possibly bite my own parents, could I? Or maybe I would try to, and they'd have to lock me in a cage, like Great-aunt Margo's bats.

And if I become nocturnal, I thought as I blindly waved to Dad and walked into West Side Prep, *will I even be able to go to school anymore?*

I realized that, soon, my fight with Gabby would seem like small potatoes compared to my new problems.

At school, Gabby and I avoided each other, which was easy to do since we had no classes together. In the classes I had with Padma and Caitlin, they looked at me with cautious expressions and said, "I hope you guys make up soon!" and "Stuff will be so awkward if you and Gab stay mad at each other!"

At lunch, I solved the problem for everyone by walking right by their table — Gabby pretended to be very involved in her tofu stir-fry — and sitting with Zora, Janie, and Matt from student council. I threw myself into discussing plans for the dance, trying to put out of my mind that Other Big Thing I'd be doing on Friday night.

I wasn't too surprised when Gabby skipped that afternoon's student council meeting. She missed out on Henry calling me Emma-Rose (again!) when he took attendance. Even Ms. Goldsmith looked a little surprised. That was the only sign, though, that Henry gave of our Saturday encounter. He was silent for most of the meeting, and so was Ashlee. She seemed run-down and stressed. Zora, Matt, Janie, and I did most of the talking. Matt told everyone how he got permission to borrow the skeleton from the science lab, and I asked people to bring in apples to fill up the cauldron.

Tuesday and Wednesday passed in much the same way. The amazing thing was that, despite my fuzzy state of mind, I was still all about the new

Emma-Rose. It seemed my abilities were actually sharpening the closer I got to my initiation. In gym class, I was still serving and spiking with incredible skill, leading Coach Lattimore to pull me aside and ask me if I would consider trying out for the volley-ball team.

But I couldn't share any of these random victories with Gabby. This was the longest we'd ever gone without talking, and it felt beyond strange.

Late Wednesday night, I was lying in bed, thinking about Gabby, and how I might lose *all* my friends once I became a creature of the night. (Though would I gain new fanged friends? I wondered.) Suddenly, I heard a key unlock the front door. I sat bolt upright. Mom and Dad had both gone to bed hours ago.

I slipped out of bed and peered into the hallway. Sure enough, Great-aunt Margo was gliding toward the guest room, her suitcase in hand. She didn't notice me.

In the moonlight coming through the windows, I saw that she looked less pale than usual. *What kind of* spa *had she been to?* I wondered. An oasis for vampires, complete with gourmet blood drinks and luxurious bat caves to sleep in? And would I go to that spa, too, when my time came?

I went back to bed and tried to stay awake to listen in on Great-aunt Margo's activities. But sleep pulled me under. I had the nightmare about the glowing eyes again, and this time the terror seemed all too real.

It's Thursday, I realized when I woke up in a cold sweat. *Student council meeting.* No wonder I'd had the nightmare. I wanted to text Gabby and tell her, but I didn't feel ready to reach out yet.

Still, I found myself hoping I would bump into my former BFF in the halls at school. During lunch, I sat with my student council friends, but I barely listened as Janie described the spooky sounds she'd downloaded to her iPod for the dance. When I glanced over my shoulder, Caitlin and Padma waved to me, but Gabby ignored me, stabbing at her salad with her fork.

When I walked into student council, I was startled to find Gabby in her usual seat in the back. Without looking at her, I took my usual seat, too. After I'd pulled out my notebook and pen, Gabby leaned over my notebook, like old times.

I think you're being immature, she wrote in her neat, precise handwriting.

I let out a huff. The nerve!

ME? I wrote back. You're the one who's turned all our friends against me.

I SO HAVE NOT! Gabby responded, the tip of her pen bleeding into the paper as her cheeks turned bright pink. *You're choosing not to sit with us at lunch!*

I snatched up my pen to write back when Ashlee called out a halfhearted "Order!" and listlessly tapped her gavel against the desk.

I couldn't help it; I glanced at Gabby, and she glanced at me, too. I knew that, despite our fight, we were wondering the same thing: if the strain of being president/princess was starting to take its toll on Ashlee Lambert.

Looking frail — but still managing a sneer in my direction — Ashlee reminded us that the dance was tomorrow, and then asked Henry to take attendance. I sat up straighter, eager for Gabby to hear Henry speak my name. But Henry, sitting in the front row with his legs stretched out in front of him, didn't get up.

"I've been thinking, Ashlee," he said. "Do we really need to take attendance at every meeting? If someone can't make it once in a while, is it that big of a deal?"

Murmurs and whispers darted through the classroom — the sound of another rebellion in the works.

Ashlee looked horrified. Once again Ms. Goldsmith mentioned the "democratic process" and asked everyone to vote on whether or not they wanted attendance taken. The only people who voted yes were Ashlee and me.

So attendance didn't happen, and Ashlee seemed so shaken up by this change that she adjourned the meeting early and flounced out with Eve. People cheered, eager to enjoy the afternoon. As I picked up my book bag, Henry appeared by my desk.

"Hey," he said to me.

"Oh, hey," I said, tucking my hair behind my ears and feeling my face turn warm.

"I just, uh, wanted to thank you," Henry said with a quick smile.

"For what?" I asked, rolling my pen back and forth between my fingers. I could practically *feel* Gabby trying to listen in.

"For inspiring me to stand up to Ashlee," Henry replied, his smile widening. "It's easy to forget that she doesn't rule the seventh grade, you know?"

I nodded, glad that Henry found me so inspiring. But was he going to keep on pretending that Saturday had never happened?

"So, are you . . . you know, ready for tomorrow?" Henry asked, dropping his voice.

"Yeah, sure," I lied, fighting down a pang of nervousness.

"Okay." Henry looked dubious. But he shrugged and put his hands in his pockets before wheeling around and walking off to meet Roger.

As soon as he was gone, Gabby tapped me on the shoulder. "What was *that*?" she whispered, her eyes huge with curiosity.

Part of me was bursting to tell her, but there were too many people around. Plus, I was still worked up from our note-writing battle.

"Nothing," I said coolly, standing. "You wouldn't believe me, anyway."

That night, it was just me and Dad for dinner. Mom and Great-aunt Margo had to stay late at the museum to prepare for the opening. As I pushed my pasta around my plate, Dad asked me what I was going to be for Halloween. (He and Mom didn't know that I'd be making an appearance at the gala.)

I realized that in all my obsessing over the Nocturne Ritual and my transformation, I hadn't picked a costume for the dance. There was no time now to prep for my Goth Hermione look. So, after dinner, I ransacked my room for other options. As I shook open my book bag, out fell two items: One was the crumpled-up confession I'd written to Henry in the library. The other was the pair of plastic fangs from Gabby.

I stood in my room, holding my letter and the fangs, and I realized that the obvious answer had been there all along.

I would dress up as myself.

Friday dawned damp and gray — perfect Halloween weather. I put on the outfit I'd planned on wearing to the gala: my black satin skirt and ruffle-front purple blouse. Since it was a West Side Prep tradition to come to school in costume, I slipped the plastic fangs in my mouth. They felt natural in there, as I knew they would. I added white powder to my cheeks to make my face even paler, put mascara on my lashes, and drew two lines of red lipstick from my mouth to my chin. I tied a black ribbon around my neck, and then looked at myself in the mirror.

I was — and wasn't — surprised at how much I resembled Great-aunt Margo. *Better get used to it*, I told myself, baring my fangs at my reflection.

"Yikes! A vampire!" Dad yelped when I entered the kitchen. He clutched his chest and pointed at me, a goofy smile on his face.

"It's okay, Dad, I'm not six years old," I said, putting down my heavy bag of decorations. "I don't take Halloween that seriously anymore."

Unless it involves an ancient vampire ritual.

"But you look very convincing, Emma-Rose," Mom said, handing me a glass of cranberry juice. "It's too bad Margo left for the museum already and couldn't see you like this! Did you know that there are all sorts of vampire legends in the town she comes from? Well, the whole region we're from, really. Isn't that funny?"

I looked at Mom. There was a whole lot I could have said in response but I decided to drink down my juice instead.

School was a maze of ghosts, superheroes, werewolves, pirates, and princesses. Ashlee Lambert was, fittingly, one of the princesses, complete with a sparkling tiara and a pouffy pink ball gown. Eve and Mallory were dressed as angels, which made me snicker. And Gabby, Caitlin, and Padma were all dressed as faeries, which totally annoyed me. There were a few other girls dressed as vampires, but as Zora — dressed as a ladybug — pointed out during lunch, none looked as authentic as me.

There was only one boy dressed as a vampire, and I bumped into him on my way to science class.

"You didn't," Henry told me, his jaw dropping as he took in my fangs, powdered face, and fake blood.

"*You* didn't," I responded, taking in *his* fangs, black cape, and fake blood.

"Hey, I had this costume planned way before last Saturday," he laughed, holding up his hands. He glanced over his shoulder and took a step closer to me. "Are you gonna wear your costume to the . . . you-know-what?" he whispered.

I shook my head. "Hopefully, I'll have time to wash off the blood before —"

"'Sup, Dracula?" Roger called, coming up to Henry. I took that as my cue to leave and walked away, wondering if Henry was still going to help me set up for the dance.

After the final bell, Zora, Janie, and Matt helped me carry all the decorations to the gym doors. Then my new friends dispersed, promising that they'd try to get out of their commitments in time to come and pitch in. Feeling heavyhearted, I assured them it was okay. Then I lifted up two of the bags and walked into the empty gym alone.

"Happy Halloween," said Gabby.

She was sitting on the bleachers, hugging her knees to her chest. Her expression was very serious — well, as serious as someone can look when their cheeks are dusted with gold sparkles and they have fake antennae on their head.

"What — what are you doing here?" I blurted, setting down my bags in shock.

Gabby stood up, her golden faerie wings fluttering. "Did you really think I wouldn't come help you?" she asked softly.

I shrugged and glanced down at my black flats. "Well, last week you said . . ."

"I said a lot of things," Gabby admitted. "Things I didn't mean."

I looked back up at Gabby, who was making her way down the bleachers. Was she actually apologizing?

"Me too," I replied. I remembered the cruel things we'd said last Friday and felt a swell of regret. Seeing Gabby here, now, made me realize how much I had missed her.

"I like your costume," Gabby said, smiling slightly.

I felt the beginnings of a smile, too. "Thanks. I think it's all about the fangs."

Gabby shook her head. "They were a thoughtless present," she said.

"No," I protested, feeling my throat tighten. "I just didn't appreciate them at the time." I realized that I'd been so quick to lash out at Gabby, when she'd been trying to help me, in her own way. "Your costume's nice, too," I offered, gesturing to her gold-sequined tank, black jeans, wings, and antennae.

"Caitlin and Padma totally ripped off my idea," Gabby said, rolling her eyes. "When we got together to plan our costumes last night, all I could think about was how much more fun it would have been with you." She looked down, biting her lip.

My eyes welled with tears. "Were you miserable this week, too?"

Gabby looked up at me, teary-eyed. "Totally," she replied, her voice wavering.

All of a sudden, I realized how silly we had been, fighting with each other. Nothing could change the fact that we were best friends. Not even my being a vampire.

Gabby must have realized the same thing because she stepped forward and threw her arms around me. We hugged tight, both of us half crying, half laughing.

"I'm so sorry!" Gabby burst out, and I patted her wings. "I'm sorry that I didn't believe you. I was a terrible best friend." She stepped back and swiped at her eyes, getting gold sparkles on her fingers.

"It's okay," I said, meaning it. I dabbed at my eyes with the back of my hand, hoping my mascara wasn't running. "I'm sorry, too. I shouldn't have gotten so mad at you. It's just that there was so much going on, both with the dance and —"

"I know!" Gabby cried. "I think you're amazing for doing the decorations. And you were right. I guess I *was* a little jealous that you were getting all this attention." She shook her head, looking remorseful. "But I'm over it. I hope you know I really *am* happy for you, Em."

Em. Hearing that name again lifted my spirits. "I know you are," I said quietly.

Gabby sniffled and adjusted her antennae. "And I feel really bad that I didn't listen to you about that *other* stuff." She lowered her voice, even though it was just us in the gym. "After we fought, I Googled vampires and Transylvania and I have to say, a lot of it *does* make sense. I even wanted to send you some links but I was too stubborn."

"I wanted to e-mail you, too," I said. "I think we're *both* too stubborn. Maybe that's why we're BFF."

Gabby and I grinned at each other. Even though I knew I had a big, scary night ahead of me, right then all I wanted to do was jump for joy.

"Okay, you need to update me," Gabby whispered, her eyes sparkling. "Any Great-aunt Margo news? I've been dying to know."

"There's some news, all right," I said, feeling butterflies swarm my stomach. As Gabby and I began taking the decorations from the bags, I told her all the latest, from what Henry and I discovered in the library to my secret mission tonight. Not once did Gabby roll her eyes. Instead, she listened carefully and gasped at the right places.

"So *that's* what you and Henry were talking about yesterday!" Gabby exclaimed when I was finished.

"Em, I can't believe you're *friends* with him now! You know what I think?" she added, smiling excitedly. "I think he likes you!"

My cheeks burned. "What? No. He's just into vampire stuff. That's why he helped me out at the library."

Gabby shook her head emphatically, her antennae wiggling. "Please. It's *so* obvious. Why do you think he teases you all the time? He's *crushing* on you."

"No way," I said firmly. "Trust me, Gab. Henry Green does not —"

Before I could finish, the gym doors swung open and a boy's voice echoed through the big empty space.

"Did you know there's a skeleton in the hallway?" asked Henry.

Gabby and I glanced at each other in horror. Had he heard us?

"I — yeah —" I stammered, caught off guard. I lowered my head so Henry couldn't see me blush. "I was supposed to bring that in."

"I'll get it," Henry said. He turned to go, his vampire cape trailing behind him. Then he glanced back at us. "Why are you guys just standing around talking?" he asked. "You haven't started putting up anything yet!"

"OMG, he's right!" Gabby gasped, glancing at the windows above the bleachers. The sky was dimming. "We have to finish in time so you can leave for the gala." She shot a meaningful look at Henry, who raised his eyebrows at her. "Yes, I know *everything*," she said, putting her hands on her hips. "I'm her best friend."

I smiled at Gabby, then reached down to tear open a bag of balloons while Henry darted back into the hallway to collect the skeleton and the rest of the decorations.

"Okay," Gabby said, pulling out the black streamers. "Operation Hollywood Halloween is in effect."

The three of us moved like a whirlwind through the gym. While Henry rolled out the red carpet and set up the spooky-sounds iPod, Gabby and I blew up balloons, hung streamers, and stuck on wall decals. Within an hour, the gym had been completely transformed. We stepped back to admire our work.

The gym now looked like the coolest haunted house ever. The smoke machine filled the air with fog, and the cackle of a zombie drifted out from the iPod's speakers. The walls were covered with sparkly decals of skulls, ghosts, and cobwebs, and on the far wall was a decal of the Hollywood sign, written out in creepy lettering. Black and orange balloons, with matching streamers, dangled from the ceiling and brushed the head of our skeleton, which stood by the entrance to greet people.

"I think it's perfect," Gabby declared, straightening out the edge of the red carpet with her toe. "All thanks to you, Em!" She applauded, which made me embarrassed.

"I couldn't have done it without you guys," I said truthfully. "And Zora, Janie, and Matt," I added.

"Maybe," Henry said, smiling. "But you're the genius who came up with it all."

I felt another blush start to take over my face, but just then Eve Epstein marched into the gym.

"*Who's* a genius?" she demanded, fixing her halo.

"Not you," Gabby muttered, and I covered my mouth to keep from giggling.

"Emma-Rose," Henry announced. "She did all this," he added, sweeping his arm to indicate the gym.

Eve looked impressed, but then she seemed to remember herself and tossed her hair over her shoulder. "It's nice enough," she said snippily. She pulled her cell phone out of the pocket of her white dress. "I'll text Ashlee and tell her it's approved."

"Where *is* Ashlee?" I asked, reaching for scissors to cut off a piece of tape.

"She had to be somewhere important," Eve replied, texting away. "She'll be arriving at the dance fashionably late."

"Really?" I asked, irritated. Ashlee had *demanded* that I show up early, and she couldn't be bothered to come? How selfish . . . and typical.

"Em," Gabby whispered, sidling up to me and touching my shoulder. She tapped her watch. "It's getting to be that time."

My heart flipped over in my chest. This was it.

"Okay," I said, putting down the scissors. "Let me just go wash off my makeup." The gala was not a costume party, and I needed to look somewhat presentable.

Gabby nodded. "Henry and I will meet you outside."

"Wait — what?" I sputtered, glancing from my best friend to Henry. "You guys are coming *with* me?"

"Of course we are," Henry said as Eve trotted off

to inspect the smoke machine. "We have to make sure you at least get inside the museum okay."

Gratitude welled up in me. I'd never known how important good friends could be. Before I could thank them, though, the gym doors banged open, and Zora, Janie, and Matt flooded inside — along with all the volunteer paparazzi, wielding cameras.

"Sorry we're late!" Zora cried, running toward me. "It looks *incredible*!"

"No, you're right on time," I said, handing her the scissors and tape. "I have to take off now, but I'll be back later."

I didn't mention that I might be coming back as a bat.

Chapter Twelve

The full moon hung low in the starry sky as Gabby, Henry, and I speed-walked the two blocks to the museum. *A blood moon*, I thought, seeing its faint reddish glow. The night had a bite of cold to it. A few of the trees in Central Park had shed their leaves, and their naked branches stretched up like skeleton arms. I shivered, wishing I'd worn a cardigan over my ruffle-front blouse.

The museum, a grand building with marble columns, looked even grander tonight. It was lit from below by floodlights, and an orange-and-black banner reading CREATURES OF THE NIGHT rippled down over the entrance. Sleek black limousines were parked out front, and women in shimmering dresses and men in tuxedoes climbed the sweeping staircase to show their invitations to the security guards.

I realized that Gabby, Henry, and I must have made a strange sight as we walked up the steps together: a handsome boy vampire, a pretty golden faerie, and a pale, trembling girl. The three of us stopped in front of the large bronze statue of Theodore Roosevelt on his horse.

"Here," Gabby said, handing me her small black purse. "I put your cell phone inside this. Call or text me if you need *anything*."

"I don't think a bat can send texts," I said, my teeth chattering.

"All right, then call us when the ritual's over," Henry whispered. "We'll come back and get you."

I felt my stomach drop out from under me. "Wait — you mean you guys won't be waiting out here?"

Gabby and Henry shook their heads, looking sorry. "We need to go back to the dance for a little bit," Henry explained. "Otherwise it might look suspicious if all three of us are gone."

"And I, um . . ." Gabby fiddled with one of her

antennae, smiling sheepishly. "I need to meet Milo at the school. I think he's there already."

For a second, I forgot all about the Nocturne Ritual. "Milo from ballet?" I squealed. "He's going to the dance?"

Gabby nodded, grinning and blushing. "On Wednesday, I went up to him after ballet class and asked if he wanted to come to West Side Prep's Halloween dance. And he said yes! You were right, Em. I just needed to be brave."

"Oh, Gab," I cried, excited for my friend. I gave her a quick hug, and Henry rolled his eyes at us, but he was smiling.

"Okay, you guys go have fun at Hollywood Halloween," I said, waving Gabby and Henry off. "Maybe I'll see you later . . . or not." I had no idea what the future held for me. As a full-fledged vampire, would I still be able to lead my old life? Go to school? Keep my friends?

"We *will* see you," Gabby said firmly, giving me another hug. "We'll stand by you no matter what happens."

Henry looked a bit embarrassed by this statement, but he nodded all the same, his green eyes holding my gaze.

"And just remember to be brave," Gabby whispered to me with a smile.

Wishing me luck, Gabby and Henry headed down the steps. Then, my heart hammering, I walked toward the museum's entrance. A fancy-looking couple ahead of me flashed the security guards their ivory-colored invitations. I didn't have an invitation, but I knew getting past the guards would be the easiest part of the night.

The guards on duty were Timothy, who used to give me lollipops when I was little, and Erica, who was very no-nonsense. As I approached them, I heard Timothy saying to Erica, ". . . and they still haven't figured out how those bat cages got open every night."

"I'm telling you, there is something weird about those bats," Erica replied.

I froze, my blood running cold. Erica didn't know how right she was. Part of me wanted to tell her and Timothy everything — to warn them about the upcoming ritual. Then Timothy spotted me and he beamed.

"Emma-Rose?" he called. "My goodness, you've grown! You haven't been by the museum in a long time."

He looked so happy to see me that I couldn't bear to tell him the truth. Instead, I tried to play it cool.

"Hi, Timothy!" I said. "Are my parents inside already? I was supposed to come with them, but I got stuck at school."

"They are indeed," Timothy said, motioning for me to pass him. "So is your great-aunt. She's *quite* a lady."

"There's something weird about her," Erica said under her breath. But when I glanced at her, she gave me a big smile. "Hey there, Emma-Rose!"

I nodded and stepped past her into the soaring lobby.

The gala was in full swing. People dressed in their finest stood chattering and sipping from champagne flutes. Classical music was playing, silver twinkle lights were twined around the columns, and waiters were carrying trays of salmon puffs and spring rolls. I spotted three movie stars and the mayor. For a moment, I let myself relax and take in the glamour of it all.

Suddenly, I caught sight of my parents, standing a few feet away. I backed up and hid behind a column. I couldn't let Mom and Dad know I was here — that would lead to too many questions. From my secret spot, I saw that Mom looked beautiful in a light green gown, and Dad looked dashing in his tux. They were nibbling on spring rolls and talking to someone I couldn't see. When the waiter blocking my view moved, I saw that that someone was Great-aunt Margo.

She was wearing a black floor-length dress with a lacy black shawl, black silk gloves, and a ruby necklace. She was laughing at something Dad was saying, as calm as the night sky outside. *So the ritual hasn't started yet*, I thought. Would there be some sort of sign when it did?

Mom began clinking a fork against her glass, calling for people to gather around. The classical music stopped playing, and a hush fell over the great hall. I stayed behind my column, praying my parents wouldn't see me.

"Good evening," Mom called. "My name is Lillian Paley, and I'm honored to welcome you to the opening of Creatures of the Night. Many people assisted in making this exhibit as informative and exciting as it could be. I'd like to acknowledge them all tonight.

First, I'm thrilled to introduce Margaret Romanescu, one of the world's leading experts on bats and taxidermy. She also happens to be my aunt!"

The crowd laughed and applauded as Great-aunt Margo came to Mom's side.

"Greetings," my great-aunt said in her thick accent. "I must say that my niece, Lilly, is a vonderful curator. Ven I suggested to her the idea for this exhibit, she took it and ran vit it."

Of course it was all Great-aunt Margo's idea! I thought, shuddering.

"You must excuse me now as I go put some finishing touches on the exhibit," Great-aunt Margo said with a small bow. "Ve vant it to be perfect. Good night!"

With that, she turned and walked past the empty ticket booths and into the heart of the museum.

My stomach jumped. *She was leaving the gala.* This was the sign. The Nocturne Ritual was going to start! And now, I knew for sure where it would be held.

I inched slowly out from behind my column, just as Mom was introducing a gray-haired man whom she called the world's leading expert on rats.

Everyone was so busy applauding that they didn't seem to see me slipping through the crowd.

I held my breath as I made my way past the ticket booths. Then I heard someone call out, "Miss?"

Oh no.

I glanced over my shoulder and saw one of the waiters watching me. "Where are you going?" he asked in the suspicious tone adults sometimes use with kids.

I thought fast. "To the bathroom," I mouthed. Then, before he could ask another question, I turned and sprinted away.

There were signs along the hall indicating where the Creatures of the Night exhibit was, and I followed them. I could only hope that there were no guards patrolling this part of the museum, and that no one but the waiter had seen me come this way.

I raced through the darkened rooms full of animal dioramas. Tonight, the stuffed wolves, bears, deer, and antelope looked menacing behind their glass panes. I dashed into one of the dinosaur rooms, where the skeletons seemed to glow like pale ghosts. I passed through the cafeteria, and finally, I reached an arched entryway with a sign that read: CREATURES OF THE NIGHT EXHIBIT STARTS HERE.

There was no turning back now.

I tiptoed through the archway, my heart pounding. The room I entered was pitch-black and ice-cold. The silence seemed to swallow me. Taking a deep breath, I wiped my clammy palms against my satin skirt and peered through the darkness. Fear snaked down my spine, but I made myself move forward. I had to do this.

And that was when it hit me:

I was living out my nightmare.

This — this very moment — was the terrifying dream I'd been having for the past month! Had the dream, in a way, also been my summoning?

Slowly, my eyes adjusted to the darkness around me. I saw the big placard on the wall that read: BATS. Sure enough, the open-topped glass cases around me contained Great-aunt Margo's "stuffed" bats. They were, once again, hanging upside down, their eyes squeezed shut, as if sleeping.

Then, one by one, the bats' eyes started to open. And, just like in my dream, they glowed bright red. Small red bat eyes. Evil eyes. Staring right at me.

One of the books I'd read in the library said that

hungry vampire bats tended to have red eyes. I started to shake uncontrollably. These bats must have been starving, but they wouldn't attack me, would they? I was one of them, or I would be soon enough.

The bats began to lift their wings, and then, as one unit, they all rose up out of their glass cases. Their black wings beat the air and their crimson eyes shone. I bit my lip to keep myself from shrieking.

I watched as the bats made a swooping turn before flying deeper into the exhibit. I knew I had no choice but to stumble after them, passing through rooms full of stuffed rats, possums, koalas, and other nocturnal creatures.

I heard faint voices coming from one of the rooms up ahead. The voices soon grew louder, and I realized that I was hearing the murmurings of people.

I stepped into the final room of the exhibit. Here, the walls were lined with posters that listed scientific facts about the creatures of the night. But the rest of the room was bare — except for the group of kids huddled in the center, all of them clutching small red cards and looking terrified.

Twelve-year-olds, I understood in a heartbeat, my eyes skimming over the ashen faces. *Fledglings. Like me.* I wasn't sure any of them saw me, though. Their gazes were fixed on the bats that had settled into the eaves of the ceiling.

One bat — the glossy, graceful bat I had seen transform into Great-aunt Margo last week — hovered in midair, facing the trembling group of fledglings. I was trembling, too, and my mouth had gone completely dry. I wondered if I should move my numb feet forward and join the group.

But before I could, the hovering bat began to morph into her human form. Her wings became arms, her claws turned into legs and feet, her ears shrunk, and her face became the face I knew so well.

And, I noticed with a lurch, there was not only one bat transforming in the room. All the other bats began to drop down from the eaves. Then, just like Great-aunt Margo, each bat grew arms, legs, hands, and feet. Bat ears became human ears, snoutlike noses became human noses, and beady red eyes became larger red eyes, until the space around the fledglings was packed with normal-size adults.

The fledglings gasped and screamed, but my own scream seemed to stick in my throat. I could only stare, gape-jawed, at the vampires before me.

They, like the fledglings, came in all shapes, colors, and sizes. There were male and female vampires; tall, skinny vampires; and short, pudgy vampires. There were vampires with fair complexions, and vampires with skin the color of cocoa. There were cruel-looking vampires who hissed and snapped at the fledglings, and there were kind-looking vampires who waved and blew kisses. Some were dressed in black, some in red, and others in yellow, orange, green, or pink. There seemed to be no single vampire look. Maybe my pale skin and my love for dark colors was just a coincidence.

But the vampires had one feature in common — they all had very long, very sharp, bright-white fangs.

I heard the sound of my own ragged breathing. Since I hadn't read more of *The Vampyre*, I had no idea what the steps of the Nocturne Ritual were. I wondered if it involved each of the fledglings being bitten by the vampires. I put my hands up to my throat, shrinking deeper into the shadows.

When all the bats had morphed into people, Great-aunt Margo clapped her hands and in a clear, booming voice, began to speak.

"As the Empress of Vampires, I am delighted to velcome you one and all to the five-hundred-and-eightieth annual Nocturne Ritual!"

I gasped. *My* great-aunt Margo was the Empress? I wasn't sure whether to feel proud or terrified.

The full-fledged vampires clapped politely, and the fledglings moved in tighter together, embracing one another.

"Do not be frightened, my dah-links!" Great-aunt Margo bellowed. "This ancient rite marks the most important moment in your young lives as creatures of the night. You have been summoned from all over the vorld to this great city to become full-fledged. May I add that it is a pleasure to return to New York after thirteen long years. Last year, the Nocturne Ritual was held in Paris, and it vas, my dah-links, an absolute mess, for reasons I vill not go into here."

The full-fledged vampires nodded and grumbled among themselves, clearly remembering Paris.

"And now!" Great-aunt Margo clapped her hands. "I vill recite the incantation."

"Most excellent," murmured a female vampire, pressing her hands together excitedly. "I cannot wait to begin the hunt tonight."

I felt sick. So when we all became bats, we'd fly off to hunt? Would I be prepared?

Great-aunt Margo raised her arms over her head, and there was a tense silence. Then she pronounced a long string of words in a melodic-sounding foreign language that I guessed was Romanian. The only word I recognized was *nosferatu.*

Vampire.

When she was finished, Great-aunt Margo lowered her arms. And suddenly, there was a shifting and a rustling among the fledglings.

One by one, they were transforming.

A thin, redheaded boy was the first to change. The crimson card in his hand fluttered to the floor as his arms became long, russet-colored wings. His legs and arms morphed into claws, his face shrunk, his ears grew, and just like that, he was a bat. A bat whose open mouth now revealed long, pointy, white fangs. Great-aunt Margo beamed.

My head spun and there was a ringing in my ears. Who was next? Me? Someone else? For the first time that night, I looked at each fledgling carefully. And saw a girl with long, white-blond hair and baby-blue eyes, wearing a sparkling tiara on her head and a pouffy pink princess gown.

My heart stopped beating for a second.

It was Ashlee Lambert.

She was shivering, and I'd never seen her look so meek. My thoughts were tumbling. Was *this* why Ashlee had looked so frail at school over the past week? Was this why she hadn't come to the gym to approve my dance decorations?

How could *she* be a vampire, too?

It seemed impossible that the blond, pastel-loving princess was truly a creature of the night. But as I watched in disbelief, the tiara slipped off Ashlee's head and fell to the floor with a clatter. My classmate's face had shrunk to bat size.

The scream that had been stuck in my throat ripped free. I dropped Gabby's purse and my cell phone fell out, hitting the floor with a loud clang.

Everyone in the room turned to stare at me. In a flash, the vampires began closing in. Their glowing red eyes were curious and their white fangs grew larger as they came nearer.

My head started spinning so fast I felt like I was

on a roller coaster. Dark spots swam before my eyes, and my knees turned so wobbly I knew I would no longer be able to stand.

Was it happening? Was I becoming a bat?

I heard a familiar voice — Great-aunt Margo's — call out my name sharply.

"Emma-Rose!"

And then everything went dark.

Chapter Thirteen

"Emma-Rose? Dah-link?"

I pried my eyes open. I was lying on my back, but there was something soft beneath my head. Great-aunt Margo was sitting beside me, her navy blue eyes worried.

Everything came rushing back: the Nocturne Ritual. Ashlee Lambert. The bats.

"Am — am I a bat?" I croaked. I tried to lift my head — it felt like my normal head — and look down at my arms, which felt like my normal arms.

"Of course not, dah-link," Great-aunt Margo said gently.

She helped me to a sitting position. We were still in the room where the Nocturne Ritual had been held, but we were alone now.

"Where are — the others?" I asked, glancing around in panic.

"They had to . . . fly off," Great-aunt Margo answered carefully. "You've been unconscious for a few minutes."

"I *fainted*?" I shook my head in surprise. I had never passed out before. "So everyone saw me?" *Even Ashlee?* I wondered.

Great-aunt Margo nodded. "It's a good thing I rushed over in time to catch you. Here, drink this." She held out a paper cup full of bright red liquid.

"What is it?" I whispered, cowering.

"Cranberry juice," Great-aunt Margo replied with a small smile. Her fangs were gone, replaced with regular white teeth. "Your mom told me it's your favorite."

"Is Mom here?" I gasped, turning around to inspect the room again.

"Shh, no," Great-aunt Margo said, patting my shoulder. "Relax. Your parents do not know about anything that happened. They are still enjoying the gala."

I stared at my great-aunt, my mind still foggy. "What *did* happen?" I asked, my voice cracking with fear and confusion.

"Drink up first, and then ve vill talk," Great-aunt Margo said.

I was still suspicious of the crimson liquid. But when I took a sip, all I tasted was pure, tangy juice. I gulped it down and immediately felt better.

"Vonderful," Great-aunt Margo said, taking the empty cup from me. "I am glad I told Edvard to run and fetch the juice from the cafeteria."

"Who's Edward?" I asked. "Was he one of the . . ." I shot a glance at my great-aunt, unsure if I could speak the word that had haunted me for the past two weeks. "Vampires?" I finished in a whisper.

Great-aunt Margo was silent for a moment, and then, very slowly, she nodded.

"So it's true," I gasped, my eyes glued to my great-aunt's face. "Everything was real. You're the Empress of Vampires?"

My great-aunt lowered her eyes modestly. "Indeed," she murmured.

I'd known the answer, but it was startling to hear her confirm it.

"And the bats you brought to New York were just pretend stuffed bats," I went on, my heartbeat picking up. "And every night you've all been flying out to

Central Park to suck the blood of squirrels and birds and raccoons, and — and . . ."

And you're a dangerous monster! I thought, inching away.

"Vait." Great-aunt Margo held up one hand, her ruby ring flashing. "Yes, my colleagues are guilty of the hunting in Central Park. But *I* only vent vit them now and then to supervise, to make sure that they did not hunt in an overly cruel manner. As the Empress, I have evolved beyond sucking the blood of animals. I am able to get my nourishment from the same food humans consume, such as rare meat."

"But do you ever consume — humans?" I whispered, hugging myself.

"Heavens, no," Great-aunt Margo assured me with a shudder. "The majority of vampires no longer attack humans. Those who do give the rest of us a bad name. The more intellectual of our breed stopped that boorish practice centuries ago."

"Wow." I let my arms fall limply to my sides. "I never knew."

"Vell, how vould you be expected to know that?" Great-aunt Margo chuckled.

I shrugged, my heart now pounding. "Because I'm like you. I'm a — I was a fledgling — a —"

"You," Great-aunt Margo cut in softly, reaching out and smoothing my hair, "are a lovely young lady who is much too curious for her own good."

I felt my brow furrow. "What do you mean?" I demanded.

There was a laugh in Great-aunt Margo's voice as she replied, "I am sorry to disappoint you, my dah-link, but you are not a vampire."

Her words were like a bucket of ice water. I blinked, hoping I wouldn't pass out again.

"But . . . no!" I exclaimed, getting unsteadily to my feet. Great-aunt Margo looked up at me calmly. "I *know* I am," I protested. "You don't have to lie to me to make me feel better. Look." I began to count on my fingers. "First of all, we look exactly alike. Second, I love rare meat, and I can't stand garlic. Third, I don't sleep at night, and I hate sunshine. Fourth, I have, like, these miniature fangs" — I pointed to my incisors — "and, fifth, *you* summoned me to the Nocturne Ritual!"

I caught my breath, glaring down at my great-aunt. Was she lying to me because I had fainted?

Because she thought I wasn't tough enough to make it as a vampire?

"If you vould sit down again, dah-link, I can explain everything," Great-aunt Margo replied, reaching up to take my hands.

Reluctantly, I let my great-aunt pull me back down to sit on her shawl.

"Ve look alike because ve are related," Great-aunt Margo began with a smile. "And it is something you should be happy about, my dear, because I vas quite attractive in my youth, if I do say so myself." She batted her lashes and patted her bun.

"But I thought vampirism is inherited," I pressed. "It's passed on through the maternal line! If I inherited your looks, why not your . . ."

"Difference?" Great-aunt Margo gave a wry laugh. "Vampirism is hereditary, but many generations can pass between vampires. For instance, after I became full-fledged, I discovered that my great-grandmother had been a vampire. And though you do not possess those genes yourself, there is a chance that vun of your children . . ." She trailed off, smiling mysteriously. "But only time vill tell."

My children? I twisted my mouth. The idea

seemed so, so far in the distant future I couldn't begin to imagine it.

"So the fact that we're Transylvanian has nothing to do with it?" I asked.

Great-aunt Margo shook her head. "No, all the vampires who vere here tonight have some Transylvanian blood in them. There are vampires all over the vorld, but vhat you saw here tonight is a purely Transylvanian custom."

I nodded, digesting this. It was weird to think that Ashlee Lambert's family was Transylvanian, too.

"Now, let's return to your list," Great-aunt Margo went on. "I am sure you know that countless people happen to enjoy a delicious rare steak, and even more people dislike garlic. Other people, especially those vit big imaginations like yours, often have trouble sleeping. Too many thoughts in here," she explained, lightly tapping my forehead with her cold fingers. "Especially as you get older, and life begins to get more complicated."

"Oh," I said softly. I had to admit that my great-aunt *was* making sense.

"It is true that vampires can be hurt by sunlight," she continued. "Ve tend to stay indoors during the daylight hours, and catch some catnaps in the afternoon. However, some vampires love sunshine, and are very sad that their condition does not allow them to spend a day at the beach. So your disliking sunny veather, my Emma-Rose, is simply part of who you are." She smiled, and added, "Just like your . . . vhat do they call them in English . . . in-scissors?" She pointed to my teeth.

"Incisors," I said, smiling. I felt them with the tip of my tongue. They were sharp as ever, but not as sharp as the vampires' fangs had looked.

"And finally, you vere *not* summoned to the Nocturne Ritual," Great-aunt Margo declared. "How you learned about it at all surprises me a great deal, but then again, you are a very surprising girl. To be summoned, vun must receive a crimson-colored note vun veek prior to the ritual. The note includes plane or train tickets, as necessary. The fledglings are instructed to keep the ritual an absolute secret. Ve have vays of learning if they have betrayed us." Great-aunt Margo ducked her eyes again.

I shivered. "I didn't receive a note," I admitted. "But I did have a dream. I dreamed about walking into the exhibit and seeing the bats' red eyes."

"Oh?" Great-aunt Margo raised an eyebrow at

me. "I vill say that many vampires are psychic. Perhaps this is the vun trait that vas passed down to you through the generations. Very interesting."

"So then maybe I'm a *little* bit vampire?" I felt a funny mix of hope and fear.

Great-aunt Margo shook her head. "If you vere, you vould have turned into a bat after I said the incantation. But you can see for yourself . . ." She gestured to me.

I glanced down at my ordinary arms and legs, at my slightly wrinkled black skirt. I ran my fingers over my ears. I was human, through and through.

"Do not look so glum, dah-link," Great-aunt Margo said, giving me a hug. "Be grateful that you are not flying outside now, learning how to hunt from the older vampires. Yes, it is possible to maintain something of a normal life as a vampire. You can, as I do, hold a job. You can travel and relax and go to a spa, like the vun I visited in Pennsylvania. You can have friends, and fall in love, and even have a family. But vun is, of course, never the same. It is a burden to be carried vit you, alvays."

There was a note of sadness in my great-aunt's

voice and I returned her embrace, touching her cold cheek with my warm one.

I thought of Ashlee in bat form, baring her fangs for the first time, somewhere out there in the dead of the night. Was she scared? I remembered how, one time last week, she'd wanted the school bathroom all to herself. Was it because she was already losing her reflection in the mirror? Or going through other frightening changes?

I had so many more questions for Great-aunt Margo. Questions about her own life, about Ashlee, about me. But at the moment, one question stood out from all the rest.

"So if I wasn't summoned, then what did you mean, last Friday, when you told me that *this* Friday would be a big night for me?" I asked. "I was sure you were talking about the Nocturne Ritual."

Great-aunt Margo tilted her head to one side, thinking, and then her eyes widened. "Ah!" she said, chuckling. "Your mother and I spent a lot of time together last veek, and she mentioned that you had your school dance tonight! I recall from my own girlhood how much fun a school dance can be. So I vas referring to the dance, my dah-link. That vas all."

I sat silently for a minute, letting everything sink in. After all that drama, I wasn't a vampire. I'd been so sure. So sure, in fact, that I'd become a new version of myself. A stronger, braver version. And maybe that hadn't been such a bad thing. Maybe I hadn't needed magic or horror or full-on fangs to change. Maybe I had just needed a little confidence and a little faith in myself.

I mean, who knew I'd ever be good at volleyball?

"Speaking of this dance," Great-aunt Margo said, glancing at her wristwatch. "You must have friends who are expecting you there, no? Perhaps you vould still like to go, if there is time. There may even be a handsome boy vaiting for you." Her eyes twinkled, and I couldn't help but blush.

"I guess I could still make it, if I hurried," I said, grabbing Gabby's black purse. I took out my cell phone and saw I had about twenty missed calls and double the amount of texts from Gabby. She must have been beyond worried.

"Come, I vill valk you," Great-aunt Margo offered, helping me to my feet. As I straightened out my skirt, she lifted up her shawl. "Ve can go out the secret entrance, so your parents do not see us."

Her arm around me, Great-aunt Margo led me through a hidden back door, into an alley that led onto 79th Street.

"When will you be going back to Romania?" I asked my great-aunt as we hurried toward West Side Prep.

"Tomorrow," Great-aunt Margo sighed. "And I am taking all my bats vit me. I vill be replacing them vit real stuffed bats for the exhibit before I go. But no vorries, dah-link," she added. "I have e-mail. You can write me vhenever you vant. Especially vhen you cannot sleep at night," she added, winking at me.

"I will," I promised. I knew I would always keep Great-aunt Margo's secret from my parents. But now that she and I could discuss it freely, I was looking forward to being in touch with her. Plus, since my genealogy project was due in two weeks, I'd have some facts to run by her.

With a quick kiss on the cheek, Great-aunt Margo dropped me off at school. Then she fluttered back into the night, back to the gala, or to wherever her vampires might be.

My thoughts still whirling, I ducked back inside the school. The hallways were deserted, but I heard loud music coming from the gym. Eager to see Gabby and Henry and all my friends, I broke into a run, pushing open the gym doors.

"Welcome to Hollywood Halloween! Smile for the camera!" someone cried, snapping my picture. Flashes blinded me, but I posed good-naturedly for the paparazzi. "What's your costume?" someone else called out.

I realized that I was no longer wearing my fangs or fake blood. I smiled and shrugged. "I'm me," I replied simply. "Emma-Rose Paley."

"Cool," one of the paparazzi said, and another one whispered to her friend, "She designed the whole dance!"

Just then, the gym doors opened behind me, and I spun around to see Ashlee Lambert. Her pink gown was a little crumpled, her tiara was askew, and her expression was small and scared. The hunt must have been over. She was back to her human form.

I couldn't begin to guess what she had been through tonight. But as she watched the cameras with terror in her eyes, I could guess what she was thinking.

"No photos! No photos, please!" I yelled, dashing forward and grabbing Ashlee's arm. Carefully, I steered her off the red carpet and away from the paparazzi.

"I — I saw you," she whispered to me, her eyes enormous. "Why were you there? You're not . . . You didn't become . . ."

"I'm not," I replied, still shocked by this fact myself. "But I . . . I know the Empress. I know all about it. And I won't tell a soul," I added before Ashlee could say anything else. "I swear. It will be our secret."

"Really?" Ashlee whispered to me. "You won't tell anyone? Not even Abby?"

"Um, who's Abby?" I asked, frowning.

Ashlee looked at me like *I* was the weird one. "Your best friend! The girl you sit next to in student council?"

"Oh," I said, giggling. *"Gabby."* Clearly, being a vampire hadn't changed Ashlee all that much. "Yeah, I promise. Not even Gabby."

"Thank you, Emma-Rose," Ashlee said, her voice sounding genuinely grateful. I was surprised when she reached out to squeeze my arm. Her hand, like Great-aunt Margo's, was ice-cold. "I can't tell any of my friends about it, so it's nice to know that I can talk to you if I need to."

"You can," I said. "I'm not sure how helpful I'll be, though."

Ashlee squeezed my arm again. "I'm sorry if I was ever mean to you, Emma-Rose. I guess I always thought you didn't like *me*."

Well, I didn't, I thought, but I kept this to myself. "It's okay," was all I told Ashlee. I knew she and I would never really be friends, but the secret we now shared would bond us in a strange way.

"Ashlee! *There* you are!"

Eve and Mallory bounded up to us, clucking over Ashlee. I took that as my opportunity to slip away.

The gym was packed, and Hollywood Halloween looked to be a success. A huge crowd was dancing, and Roger was goofily darting in and out of the fog from the smoke machine. Zora, Janie, and Matt were clustered around the cauldron, bobbing for apples. Kids were eating candy corn and posing for the paparazzi. Padma and Caitlin were dancing with some girls from the soccer team, and they waved to me, grinning. I waved back.

Then I spotted Gabby and Henry standing by a bowl of candy corn, both of them leaning over

Gabby's cell phone. I was sure that Gabby was texting me again, so I pushed through the throngs and rushed over to her.

"I'm here! I'm alive!" I cried. Gabby looked up from her phone and her face brightened. She gave me a huge hug.

"We were freaking *out*!" she exclaimed, stepping back to look me up and down, as if to make sure I was in one piece. "Why didn't you call or text us?"

"How was it?" Henry asked, his expression concerned. "Did it hurt to transform? Did you have to hunt right away?"

I laughed, shaking my head. "Guys," I said. "I promise I'll tell you all the details later, but it turns out I'm not a vampire after all."

"You mean you're still a fledgling?" Henry asked, furrowing his brow.

"No," I said. "I never was a fledgling. And I'll never be full-fledged. It was all in my own head."

Henry's eyes widened, and Gabby's mouth fell open. I hoped Gabby wouldn't say *I told you so*. Instead, she asked, "What about Great-aunt Margo? Is *she* a vampire?"

"Oh yeah," I said, smiling. "Though it's top secret."

Gabby and Henry nodded solemnly.

"I just can't believe you're not a vampire," Gabby said to me.

"I thought you couldn't believe I *was* a vampire," I replied, reaching out to wiggle one of her antennae.

Gabby shrugged. "What can I say? You convinced me."

I was going to tease her about that when a tall, African-American boy came over. He was cute, with big brown eyes, and he was dressed like a pirate.

"Hey, Gabby?" he said. "Is this, um, the friend you've been waiting for?"

"Oh!" Gabby giggled, looking flustered. "Yeah! Milo, this is my best friend, Emma-Rose. Em, this is Milo."

The famous Milo! I smiled at him, and he smiled back. I noticed that he had silver braces on his teeth — something Gabby would have in common with him soon!

Milo looked at Gabby again. "So, um, now that she's here, is it cool if we dance?" he asked.

Gabby peeked at me, and I gave her a subtle nod of approval. With that, she and Milo walked out onto the dance floor. I watched them, truly excited for Gabby.

Then I turned to Henry. We stood there, facing each other, and suddenly I felt tongue-tied and awkward.

"So," Henry said. He gave me a shy smile. A really nice smile. I noticed that he'd removed his fangs.

"So," I said, shifting from one foot to the other. "Now that you know I'm not a vampire, am I just a boring regular person?"

"You?" Henry shook his head, laughing. "You could never be boring, Emma-Rose."

My stomach jumped a little. I remembered what Gabby had said to me before the dance, about Henry liking me. Was she right? And did I like him?

Maybe it was time to finally admit that I did.

"So," Henry said again, extending his hand. "Since you're not a bat or a vampire, would you maybe want to dance?"

I nodded, my heart swelling. "That sounds great," I replied.

I was totally nervous — even more nervous than I'd been at the Nocturne Ritual — and Henry seemed a little nervous, too. But he took my hand and we headed onto the dance floor. The DJ was playing an old song called "Monster Mash," and soon Henry was spinning me around and we were laughing together.

As we danced, I happened to glance out one of the windows above the bleachers. Against the full October moon, I could have sworn I saw the black outline of a bat in flight. Maybe it was Great-aunt Margo. Maybe it was a different vampire. Maybe it was a regular old bat, minding its business and flying around New York City.

Or maybe, I thought with a smile, it was just my imagination.

BITE INTO THE NEXT POISON APPLE,
IF YOU DARE. . .

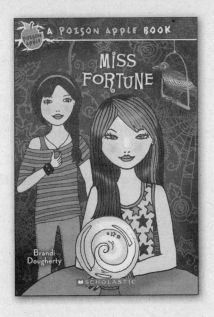

The girls staggered off the Kamikaze, Zoe grinning wildly and Mia looking a little green, and headed in the direction of the parking lot to meet Zoe's dad. Zoe was surprised by how empty the fairgrounds seemed all of a sudden. She glanced at her watch. It wasn't even 9:30 yet, but it seemed much later. The moonless sky was so cloudy, Zoe could barely make out any stars.

"Are they turning off the lights already?" she asked Mia.

Mia looked around. "I don't think so."

The grounds looked darker to Zoe somehow. It wasn't the bright and lively scene it had been just a few minutes before. A layer of exhaust blew and curled across the dirt from a nearby hot-dog stand, casting shadows in front of the girls as they walked. Zoe shivered and zipped up her hoodie. She suddenly felt a little uneasy, but she couldn't figure out why.

As they neared the edge of the carnival, just before the gated exit to the parking lot, Zoe noticed a tent she hadn't seen when they'd come in earlier that night. It looked like a big, dark cloud hovering over the entrance. Zoe thought her eyes were playing tricks on her. She could swear something was moving inside.

Just as Zoe was about to point out the tent to Mia, a woman stepped out of the shadows. Zoe jumped back, startled.

"Good evening, girls," the woman said, though her heavy accent made the words sound more like "*Good evunning, gulls.*" The woman had light olive skin and thick, dark eyebrows. She wore a black floor-length sheath dress and tattered leather sandals. A massive bun of black hair with a few streaks of gray was piled on top of her head.

"I am the Great Serafina," the woman said, gesturing toward the opening of the tent. "Would you like to have your fortunes read?"

Zoe and Mia exchanged glances and giggled nervously.

"Um, that's okay," Mia responded. "We have to go."

"I'll do them for free since the carnival is about to close for the evening," the woman offered.

Zoe surveyed the woman's face closely. Her eyes were a weird yellow and looked almost translucent, like you could see right through them. But the hint of a smile danced on her thin, pursed lips, making her seem friendly despite her intense eyes. Still, there was something a little strange about her. But at the same time, she was offering to read their fortunes for free, so that seemed pretty nice.

"Um, okay," Zoe agreed. Zoe didn't really believe in fortune-telling or magic, but she thought it might be fun. Plus, she was always looking for ideas for her next film, and she never knew where she might find them.

Mia checked her watch anxiously. "Zoe, what about your dad?"

"He'll wait," Zoe said. Once something was set in her mind, Zoe always had to follow through. "Come on, it will be funny!"

The Great Serafina bristled at Zoe's comment, but Zoe didn't notice. She just strode right into the tent. Mia hesitated, but then sighed and jogged over to duck inside behind Zoe.

The tent was small. There were burning candles everywhere, and the scent of them hung thick in the air. Zoe sneezed loudly. There was a warm, almost cozy feeling to the small space, but when Zoe studied her surroundings more closely, there was something kind of creepy about it, too. The single cot and the low stand holding a hot plate and a jug of water seemed normal enough, but the row of antique-looking bottles filled with strange liquids and plants seemed a little odd. But just as soon as she'd thought it, Zoe laughed to herself and brushed it off. *That stuff is all for show. There's no way any of this is real.*

A small folding table and two chairs were positioned in the center of the room. The table was covered with a black tablecloth and was bare except for a row of melting candles on one side.

Serafina held out a chair and motioned for Mia to sit down. Mia glanced nervously at Zoe before taking a seat. Zoe smiled and winked at Mia, which was what she always did when she was trying to make Mia feel more at ease.

"Now, let's see what the cards can tell us, shall we?" said the woman, her face bathed in candlelight. She rested a pair of thick-rimmed glasses on her nose and shifted a deck of cards between her hands. The cards seemed to have appeared out of nowhere. Zoe stood directly over Serafina's right shoulder. She made a face at Mia and giggled.

"Maybe she'll tell you who you're gonna have for math next year, Mia," Zoe giggled again. She couldn't seem to stop laughing now — it all seemed so silly.

Serafina narrowed her catlike eyes over her glasses and stared back at Zoe for a long breath.

Mia watched the woman's expression. "Zoe, shhhhh."

"What?" Zoe asked innocently. "You don't like math. . . . It was a joke." Zoe wondered why Mia was taking this so seriously. The woman was obviously a fake. Everything about the tent seemed like it was set up as an act. *Well, everything except that weird snake head*, Zoe thought to herself as she noticed a mounted snake head with outstretched jaws nestled on a piece of red satin in the corner of the tent. A small, ominous-looking bottle of liquid was propped between the snake's jaws. The snake didn't look fake. In fact, it looked pretty real. And creepy.

"Have you had your cards read before?" The woman ignored Zoe and focused on Mia.

"Um, no," Mia replied quietly.

"Well, I come from a long line of Italian fortune-tellers," said Serafina. "You will not be disappointed."

Zoe giggled again, and the woman darted her eyes in Zoe's direction once more.

"Let's begin."

Serafina's long, bony fingers slowly laid a tarot card on the table. After a minute of silence, she began.

"You will start a new journey soon," she said to Mia in a low voice.

"Yeah, seventh grade," Zoe mumbled under her breath. This time the woman turned all the way around in her chair and shot Zoe a glare. As soon as their eyes met, Zoe felt her insides turn to ice. The uneasy feeling she'd had outside the tent came flooding back. At first the woman had seemed nice and friendly enough, but when she glared at Zoe, there was something scary about her eyes. It was almost as though she was looking straight into Zoe and reading her thoughts. Zoe decided to stop joking around.

Serafina turned her attention back to Mia and placed another card on the table. "This journey, while not easy, will reap long-term happiness." She smiled warmly at Mia, and Zoe could see Mia relax a little in her chair.

Serafina tapped her bloodred fingernail on the next card she put down. "Your passion in life will serve you well."

Mia beamed. "I want to be a dancer!"

The woman returned Mia's smile and nodded. "And you shall."

At the end of the fortune, the woman handed Mia a small coin with a pyramid on it.

"This, dear, shall seal your fortune," she told Mia as she placed the coin in her palm and folded Mia's fingers over it. "Always carry it with you."

"Thanks!" Mia said brightly. "Looks like it's gonna be a good year. Your turn, Zoe!"

Serafina turned again in her chair and watched intently as Zoe made her way around the table to the other waiting chair. Zoe hurried to the chair and sat down. She hated to admit it, but she was actually a little excited to hear her fortune now that Mia's had been so fun.

The woman cleared her throat and set the first card down.

"Hmmm," she said as a small smile crept onto the edge of her thin lips. "It appears that you will make a bad decision."

"Uh, okay," Zoe laughed nervously. What a weird thing for the woman to tell her!

"Zoe, be serious." Mia poked her in the back.

The woman placed another card down and shook her head slightly. "This decision may lead to some regrettable events."

"Hey!" Zoe interrupted. She wasn't feeling so excited anymore. "Mia's fortune was way better!"

Serafina took off her glasses and set them on the table. "Excuse me?" she said slowly.

"Zoe . . ." Mia started.

Zoe's pulse quickened a little as Serafina stared at her, but she continued anyway. "Mia's was way better. How come mine is just bad stuff?"

"Do you think I'm just making this up?" The woman flicked her hand in the air and her voice rose with irritation.

"Well, I just . . ." Zoe stumbled. "Why can't mine be good, too?"

Serafina let a long slow breath escape from her lips. It sounded like the air leaking out of a bike tire, or like a snake hissing. "Would you like me to finish or not?"

"I guess so," Zoe said, though she wasn't sure she really *did* want her to continue.

The woman quickly placed the next card on the table. This time a dark look crossed her face.

"Well, your outlook has not improved. It seems as though you may be in some danger if you're not careful."

"Oh no, Zoe!" Mia gasped.

Zoe shifted awkwardly in her chair. Now she really wanted to get out of the tent, but she waited for Serafina to continue.

The woman sat perfectly still and continued to

stare at the cards on the table. Zoe waited tensely for her to speak. After another minute of silence, Zoe cleared her throat. "Um, is that it?" she asked tentatively.

Serafina suddenly lifted her gaze and locked eyes with Zoe. Zoe's pulse quickened as she waited for the woman to say something, but she just stared straight through Zoe with that same glassy expression.

"Zoe, I think we should go," Mia whispered nervously.

Zoe nodded, her voice caught in her throat. Serafina's behavior wasn't making any sense, and Zoe was starting to think that Serafina's act was more creepy than funny. Zoe moved to get up when suddenly Serafina stood and walked abruptly to Zoe's side of the table. She faced Zoe, her catlike eyes piercing right through her. Zoe stood up slowly and felt the space of the tent tighten around her. She felt dizzy. Why was the woman acting so weird?

"I must give you something to seal your fortune," the woman finally said in a monotone voice, a creepy smile edging her lips again. She raised her hands and closed her fingers around the leather cord of the necklace she was wearing. She held the necklace out in front of her and moved to place it around Zoe's neck with a robotic motion. Zoe froze.

"What are you doing?" she asked, wide-eyed. Something came over Zoe. Her arms and legs felt heavy. She had no choice but to let Serafina put the necklace around her neck.

"I am bestowing the power of the snake eye on you," Serafina replied mechanically as she waved her left hand in front of the necklace. *"Il potere dell'occhio di serpente . . . il potere dell'occhio di serpente . . . il potere dell'occhio di serpente."*

All the color drained from Zoe's face. What was with the weird chanting? Zoe wasn't sure, but she thought the words might have been in Italian. She glanced at Mia. Her friend's face was an ashy gray color. Mia looked terrified.

"I . . . I can't take this," Zoe said with a shake of her head. She reached up to remove the necklace, but Serafina's hand shot out to stop her.

"You have no choice," the woman said eerily. "The snake eye has chosen. It is yours."

"Zoe, we'd better go before your dad gets worried." Mia shifted nervously from one foot to the other. She had her hand on the opening of the tent and was already stepping outside.

Zoe could hear the tension in Mia's voice. "Yeah, okay." She backed away from the woman and took a wide step around her to get to the opening of the tent.

Once Zoe was outside, she took a deep breath. The air was surprisingly cold, but Zoe felt like she could finally breathe again. She looked down at the necklace. The tarnished silver pendant looked like a tightly coiled snake that had formed the shape of an eye. In the center of the eye sat a large red jewel. The necklace looked very old and seemed to weigh a hundred pounds. Zoe could feel the weight of it around her neck. The snake on the necklace was a little disturbing, but there was something about it that she liked. She touched the stone with her finger and felt her whole body grow warm.

She turned to look at the tent, wondering if she should try again to give the necklace back — even though for some weird reason she kind of wanted to keep it. Serafina was standing in the opening with the flicker of candlelight around her. The shadows on the tent behind her looked like giant flames on the wall.

Suddenly, Serafina called out to Zoe. "Good luck," she said in the same deep, monotone voice.

Then she threw her head back and laughed. The sound was evil and earsplitting.

A serious chill zinged down Zoe's spine. The candles made it look like the woman's eyes were glowing like firelight, too. Zoe turned and ran toward her dad's car. Mia was already waiting inside.

candy apple books
read them all!

Drama Queen

I've Got a Secret

Confessions of a Bitter Secret Santa

Super Sweet 13

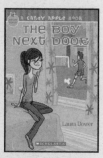

The Boy Next Door

The Sister Switch

Snowfall Surprise

Rumor Has It

The Sweetheart Deal

The Accidental Cheerleader

The Babysitting Wars

Star-Crossed

www.scholastic.com/candyapple